DESERT DEATH

The woman scrambled back along the ground. "You ain't goin' nowhere," Lavery grimaced. "I'm gonna stick this needle right through you, just like you did to him. 'Cept for you it's gonna take longer, a lot longer." He started for her.

The muscles in Garrett's face knitted tightly together. Dakota understood what the change of expression meant. He wheeled and ran for their weapons. Simultaneously, Garrett threw back the flap of his jacket and pulled the knife from its sheath. He snapped his arm. The gleaming steel ripped through the air . . .

Mitchell Dana

Incident
In A
Texas Town

AVON
PUBLISHERS OF BARD, CAMELOT, DISCUS, EQUINOX AND FLARE BOOKS

INCIDENT IN A TEXAS TOWN is an original publication of
Avon Books. This work has never before appeared in any form.

AVON BOOKS
A division of
The Hearst Corporation
959 Eighth Avenue
New York, New York 10019

ISBN: 0-380-00211-6

First Avon Printing, January, 1975.

AVON TRADEMARK REG. U.S. PAT. OFF. AND
FOREIGN COUNTRIES, REGISTERED TRADEMARK—
MARCA REGISTRADA, HECHO EN CHICAGO, U.S.A.

Printed in the U.S.A.

CONTENTS

One

The Jab of a Needle

"Garrett . . ."

The man stirred. The youth's voice, which at first reached his ears as a muffled whisper, became louder, more persistent as it summoned him from bottomless sleep to semiconsciousness.

"Wake up, Garrett . . ."

The man opened his eyes. In the profound, jarring instant when he saw the hazily outlined figure hovering above him, he threw back the blankets and grabbed for the holster which he kept at arm's reach beside him on the ground.

The youth caught him gently back by the shoulder. "No, it's all right."

Garrett stopped. The harsh morning light, flooding his senses, brought recognition. His hand moved from the gun. Groggily, he sputtered out the words, "What is it, Dakota?"

The sixteen-year-old half-turned from him and cocked his head. He said in a quiet, meaningful voice, "Listen."

Garrett gave him a strange look. He sat up and fixed his attention on the new day, trying to penetrate its fuzzy semblance of stillness. Gradually, as the dullness of sleep dropped away, he became aware of something echoing in the distance. Carried along by the gusts of the crisp autumn wind, a series of short, barking reports were resounding across the empty badlands.

Garrett's weathered face narrowed. "Gunfire," he muttered.

Dakota nodded. "About a mile off."

Slowly, yet with each movement precise, unwasted, Garrett pulled on his boots, hauled himself to his feet, and began folding his scattered bedroll.

"Garrett?" Dakota asked, surprised by the man's apparent unconcern. "Don't you think we should go find out what it's all about?"

"I don't see that it's a matter of whether we should or not," Garrett said in an easy tone, setting down the neatly rolled blankets. "That doesn't come into it one way or the other."

"Do you *want* to, then?"

"Want to?" said the man. He strode to the center of camp and picked up a metal pot which was resting on a rock near the dying fire. "Now that's something else altogether."

"Well, do you?" Dakota asked with a trace of urgency. The rapid volleys of gunfire, ringing in his ears, were beckoning him to their source.

Garrett poured the stale remnants of the previous night's coffee over the glowing embers of the campfire. He stared at the sparks spiraling upward from the charred wood. They climbed, danced in mid-air, and then, unable to climb any higher, fell and died. Garrett turned. "You do, don't you?"

"Yes," replied the youth.

"You're in the mood for some excitement, is that it? Things have been a little too quiet for you lately?"

"Could be."

"All right, then, let's get everything together and move on."

"But what about you? Do *you* want to?"

"You know, you're still going to be standing there asking questions and I'll be ready to go," Garrett said, and started for the other side of camp.

Dakota smiled. He knew this was just the reply he deserved.

"Now come on and give me a hand," the man was saying. "Whatever's going on out there, it sure's not going to keep up all day."

Dakota gave a quick toss of his head. Side by side, they walked to their saddles, hoisted them from the ground to their shoulders, and trudged over to the horses.

When they were finished breaking camp, Garrett went back to where his bedroll had been. Lying in a coil beside his gun belt was a second belt, wide and black, with an empty sheath dangling from the end nearest the brass buckle. He reached down for it and fitted it around his waist. He then picked up his knife, inspected its sharp, silvery blade a moment, and dipped it into the sheath. Next came the gun belt, which he slipped around him, setting it at an angle over the other belt so that the holster sat well below his right hip. It was a swivel holster; fixed squarely in the smooth, leathery case was a sawed-off shotgun.

After checking the twin barrels of the loaded gun and testing the swivel action of the holster, Garrett swung a vest around his shoulders, smoothed and settled it into place over the white shirt, and buttoned it tightly against his chest. He then put on a jacket—the final match to his pants, vest, and string tie—which hid the knife, but allowed the holster to hang free.

Clad in black, fully armed, Garrett picked up his hat and turned.

"Ready?" he asked.

Dakota was strapping on his six-gun. "Just a ..." he murmured absently. Absorbed in his preparations, he shifted the holster about until it felt comfortable. Then, steadying himself as if he were squaring off against some unseen opponent, he snapped up the gun.

"You're getting faster every day," Garrett said. "I'm going to have to watch out for you. You're catching up with me."

"Damn right, Garrett." His bright, purposeful eyes flashing, Dakota gave the chambers a quick spin and dug the pistol back into its holster. His expression changed; he returned the man's smile. "Damn right."

He moved for the horses. "Let's go," he called over his shoulder.

They tightened the cinches on their gear, swung themselves up into the saddles, and slapped the reins.

The man and youth urged on their horses and broke into a swift gallop. They rode headlong into the wind, which was blowing down from the east, sweeping unhindered across the vast badlands. Gray, shapeless masses of low-hanging clouds rolled through the sky and receded quickly overhead. The loosely packed earth and ever-restless tumbleweed, also subject to the wind's sway, flew backward beneath the horses' charging hooves, tossed and scattered across the land in a haze of dust. The sharp, intermittent gusts slapped and stung the faces of the two riders reproachfully, as if reminding them in the absence of the cloud-hidden sun that the proper course of nature—and of men and history as well—was westward, not eastward. But Garrett and Dakota, caught up in the exhilaration of motion, held to their path. Their bodies arched forward until they seemed to be one with their horses, they raced along the desolate stretches, drawn onward by the gunfire which rang defiantly against the profound stillness of the land.

They drew to a halt at the base of a group of rocks.

"We're getting closer," Dakota said.

"Yeah," answered the man. "It sounds like it's coming from over the rise."

Garrett led the way; they started up the narrow trail leading through the rocks.

When they reached the crest, they found spread before them a broad valley bordered on the north and south by barren, rolling hills, and on the west, where they were, by boulder-strewn slopes. To the east there opened a flat, dust-blown panorama which stretched off starkly into the overclouded horizon.

Garrett and Dakota glanced at each other in surprise. There were no signs of trouble; the gunfire was still coming from somewhere in the distance.

They scanned the valley a second time, vainly trying to locate the source of the reports, whose echoes, ricocheting from one empty hillside to the next, were lingering in the air long after the original shots had been fired. Their eyes came to rest on a cabin just beneath their view, huddled close to the foot of the rocks. Adjacent to the cabin was a small corral in which six horses were darting skittishly about, frightened by the rapid thundering sounds.

It was at this secluded outpost that the local stage line made an hour stopover on its runs, during which time the teams would be changed and the passengers would find the opportunity to eat and rest before continuing the arduous journey. Hidden away in eastern New Mexico, among

10

lands once roamed by bands of Navaho and Mescalero, the solitary cabin looked as withered and desolate as the miles of dusty wilderness that surrounded it.

In the eyes of those who drove the stages, the way station was a midway point between two extremes. In one direction lay the thriving regions of Texas, Oklahoma and Kansas; in the other were the wasted stretches of the Southwest. One never had to ask the passengers stopping here which way they were headed: the expressions on their faces told all.

Dakota had studied the cabin only a moment when his eyes quickly rose. He edged forward in the saddle.

"Listen," he said, training his ears on the harsh gunfire, "it's getting louder."

Garrett nodded distractedly. His attention had been caught by a solitary figure—a woman—who was standing before the cabin. Her hair, long and ill-kempt, was white with age. Her shrunken body was draped in a worn and billowy black dress. The dismal light lent her an alien, spectral appearance; she seemed entirely out of place in her surroundings.

Yet there was something else about her which held Garrett's gaze. It lay in the attitude of composure she maintained as she listened to the approaching gunfire. Arms folded across her chest, her stance erect and rigid, almost trancelike, she showed no signs of fear or surprise at what was happening. It was as if she had expected—had *always* expected—this to take place, and was merely waiting for impending events to run their course.

"Look, Garrett," said Dakota. "They're coming this way!"

Garrett turned his eyes away from the woman and peered across the open vista. A stagecoach had appeared from behind one of the hills in the north. The driver was furiously flailing the four-horse team with his whip and reins. The man riding shotgun had flattened himself across the top of the stage and was wheeling his carbine this way and that, firing into the distance behind him. The passengers inside the coach had also taken up the defense. Heads and arms were protruding through the open windows in tangled confusion. In each trembling, backward-bent hand was a blazing pistol.

The stage was nearing the middle of the slope when the pursuers first came into Garrett and Dakota's view. Four horsemen came charging over the top of the rise from different directions, whooping wildly, exultantly, as they squared their rifles against their shoulders and returned the others' fire, closing in on their quarry.

"What should we do?" Dakota asked.

"Come on," Garrett said, about to start down into the valley.

Amid the roar of six-guns and rifles, a voice suddenly grated, "Hold it right there. You two ain't goin' nowhere."

Garrett and Dakota spun in their saddles. Hands poised near their holsters, they looked at the boulders which loomed up around them.

"You can't see me, but I kin see you," the voice continued. "Take my word for it, I kin see you ree-ul good. And I got a rifle here aimed at botha your heads. The first one of you what tries somethin' is gonna have his brains splattered on the ground. So be real careful like and do what I tell you."

"Hey, listen—" Garrett began.

"Save it for later," came the sharp reply. "Now just shut up and git yer hands away from those guns."

Garrett and Dakota exchanged glances.

"Y'hear me? Up in the air!"

The man and youth frowned. Their arms slowly rose.

"Now fold 'em behind your heads."

Again they followed the strident command.

"Okay, keep lookin' straight ahead of you and don't turn around. Stay that way till I tell you different. Remember, I'll be watchin' you all the time."

The disembodied voice drifted away into silence. It was as if the boulders themselves had been speaking. But the only sounds which now issued from the rocks were those which had been droning steadily for the past five minutes. The massive formations of stone were reverberating, almost quaking, with the bursts of gunfire from below.

Holding themselves stiffly in the awkward posture imposed on them, Garrett and Dakota tried to inch around and catch a glimpse of the person who had gotten the drop on them. But they saw nothing—only boulders. Gradually they resigned themselves to their position and

12

shifted their gazes to what was taking place at the northern end of the valley. Like the woman who was still rooted to her place before the cabin, they were now mere spectators, separate and uninvolved. A strange, unnerving distance stood between them and the scene about to unfold.

The driver of the stage had sighted the way station, the refuge he had been racing toward since the ambush began. He lashed the horses mercilessly, in a last, desperate effort at escaping the swarm of bullets. The stage sped headlong down the hillside.

At the bottom of the slope one of the wheels struck a rock. The coach pitched into the air. When it came crashing down against the level land of the valley, there was a short snap of splintering wood. The wagon tongue broke apart from the base of the coach. The horses, though still harnessed to the long wooden beam, were free of their burden. They made a sudden turn and bolted away from the stage. The driver went hurtling forward from his seat. Face-down, his arms tautly outstretched, he rolled and tossed against the hard, dusty earth, pulled along in the wake of the terrified team. He was dragged well over fifty yards before he managed to release his grip on the reins. His limp, bleeding body tumbled to a stop. He tried to pick himself up, but slumped over instead and fell unconscious.

Lying in a prone position, firing at his attackers, the man stationed atop the coach was unaware of what had happened. When he turned to shout something to the driver, his features froze. He stared vacantly at the empty driver's box, then at the horses, which were running an aimless, frenzied course, charging toward the open plains that lay to the east. Simultaneous with his realization of the situation he was in, the stage hit another group of stones. The front axle snapped in two; one of the wheels came off and rolled into a gulley. The man was sent flying into the air. A moment later he found himself on the ground, lying in the path of the four horsemen, who were by now only a few paces behind. He scrambled for his carbine, which had fallen with him and now lay several yards away. The rider nearest him raised his rifle and fired. The man's right leg collapsed beneath him. He uttered a short cry, limped a few more steps toward his gun, and then stumbled over. Helpless, flat on his back, he looked up in time to see the rider, who was wearing a savage, toothless grin, snap the reins and bear down on him. The man's screams were lost in the thunder of the horse's trampling hooves. The other riders let out a series of rabid, hooting cheers.

Garrett and Dakota fought the impulse to go for their guns. Their upraised arms stiffened.

The passengers were now on their own. Buffeted from all sides, thrown against one another, they were trapped inside the runaway vehicle. They fired haphazardly at the four horsemen, unable to hold themselves or their pistols steady. The desperate volleys were consistently off the mark.

Horseless and driverless, tottering on its three wheels, the coach sped onward, impelled by its momentum in the direction the driver had last steered it, toward the way station. But the rough, uneven contours of the land prevented it from reaching its destination. There was a sharp jolt, a violent lurch. The springs broke loose of their hinges; the rear wheels, which had been supporting the bulk of the weight, gave way and flew off. The coach crashed to the ground, slid a short distance further on its belly, then stopped.

The passengers were stranded. Their only hope was the cabin which stood before them in the corner of the valley, a final refuge.

They never got a chance, though, to attempt—or even contemplate—the run for cover. Before they could consider what to do, the horsemen charged across the windblown landscape, quickly closing the remaining distance, and surrounded the crippled stagecoach. The ambushers went about their murderous business with sportive zest. They shot from the waist, their rifles held near the saddle at a jaunty, effortless tilt. Snorting jeeringly at their prey, they circled the stage and answered the others' gunfire with a storm of well-placed bullets. One by one, the pistols dropped from the passengers' hands. The four horsemen snarled and hissed through gritted teeth, worked up to a bloodthirsty frenzy. They tightened the circle and fired point-blank into the windows of the coach. In the angry blasts of hot lead their taunting shouts sounded like a shrill, chilling chorus of lupine howls.

Garrett and Dakota sighed and let their eyes fall.

One of the horsemen called out to the others. They lowered the smoking rifles, shoved them into their saddle holsters, and dismounted. The last thundering echo died away into the distance. The land was plunged into silence.

The two unwilling observers squirmed uneasily about. Their faces drawn and pallid, they looked as though they had just wakened from a bad dream.

Once again the scratchy-sounding voice came drifting down to them from the rocks. "Okay, you two, drop your hands," it ordered. "But do it slow, nice 'n slow."

Garrett and Dakota unlocked their fingers; the numb, blood-drained arms made an unhurried descent to their sides.

"Now your gun belts."

Garrett glanced around warily, trying to catch something out of the corner of his eye. But there was still nothing to see. His hand inched toward the sawed-off shotgun.

"I said the gun belts, mister," the voice warned. "Leave yer gun where it is."

Garrett scowled. He nodded resignedly to Dakota. They undid the buckles. The holsters, strapped on only a short while before, fell to the ground.

"And don't think I can't see that rifle of yours, mister. Drop it!"

Garrett turned and yanked his carbine from its saddle holster. Dakota looked at him thoughtfully. He knew that there was a remaining weapon, one which the ambusher could *not* see. It lay hidden beneath his companion's long black jacket. Garrett answered him with a similarly significant look which said that he, too, was thinking about the knife. Holding the carbine by the stock, he leaned over and tossed it down beside the other guns.

"Good, good. That about does it." The voice was suddenly different; it was broken with derisive cackles.

There was a quick rustle of boots and clothing scraping against stone. Garrett and Dakota swung around.

First to appear from behind one of the boulders was the long barrel of a Winchester. A moment later came the head, then the lank body of a youth is his mid-teens,

15

scarcely older than Dakota. His features were hard and brutish, oddly disproportionate. His left eye was turned at a harsh, grotesque angle. This was the eye he watched his captives with, his face set in another direction. The other eye, the normal-looking one, stared uselessly ahead of him, fixed on some vague, empty point in space.

Cautiously he grabbed hold of the rock. With one agile, upspringing motion, he was atop the boulder. Squaring his stance, he brought up the rifle and leveled it at the two figures beneath him. His face turned as if he were looking at someone standing at his side, he began sizing up his catch. The twisted, birdlike eye skipped back and forth, jumping between Garrett and Dakota. His lips gradually drew back into a wide, misshapen grin.

"So how'd you like it?" he said. "Pretty good show they put on, huh?"

"Yeah," Garret answered.

"I bet you're real glad you was just watchin'. Mighty lucky for you you wasn't down there while all that was hap'nin'."

"Yeah," Garrett said again. He poised himself tensely, waiting for the chance to go for his knife. "Mighty lucky."

"Well, I reckon you got me to thank for that," the cross-eyed youth grimaced. "Without me, who knows what mighta happened t' you two."

His leering sniggers were cut short by one of the four men in the valley below, who shouted, "Hey, Willy! What the hell's goin' on up there?"

The youth's face made a slight sideward shift. But it was only for an instant. His crooked, miscast gaze darted back to Garrett and Dakota. "Paw," he called, the Winchester steady in his hands, carefully trained on the two, "we've got ourselves some comp'ny."

"I can see that, boy," the other hooted back. "Who the blazes are they?"

"How should I know, Paw? They just rode in this way," Willy droned in response. As he spoke, the bird eye swung hurriedly from side to side. Garrett watched him closely, but was unable to tell at any given moment whether the youth was looking at him or not. He left the knife where it was.

16

"But there's nothin' to worry about," Willy was saying. "They ain't givin' me any trouble."

"I can see that, too," his father snorted. "Else we woulda been up there by now."

"Yeah, yeah. Well, what d'you want me to do with 'em?"

There was a brief pause before Willy received a reply. The four men huddled together and began talking over the matter. It did not take long for them to reach agreement. There was a quick nod from each of them, and the father looked up and called out, "Send them on down, Willy-boy!"

Garrett and Dakota felt a sudden emptiness gnaw at them. They understood what the answer meant. Their role as spectators had come to an end.

"Okay, you heard him," said Willy. "Get movin'!"

The man and youth looked at each other. They raised their reins, gave them a short snap, and slowly started forward.

A short way down the narrow trail, they heard a quick succession of thuds coming from behind them. They turned. Willy had tucked the Winchester under his arm and was climbing down from his place of ambush, making his way toward the surrendered guns of his captives. He bounded from boulder to boulder swiftly, surefootedly, like a predatory mountain cat, at home among the rocks. When he reached the trail, he knelt over the weapons, his interest caught by Garrett's sawed-off shotgun. He held the swivel holster close to the one useful eye, inspected it with curiosity, and then glanced up. Noticing that the two riders had slowed their pace, he growled, "Keep movin', keep movin'," and returned to the strange looking gun.

"He's one of them, isn't he?" Dakota said as he and Garrett continued down the rock-lined path.

"Sure seems it," the man replied.

"Then what was he doing up there? Why wasn't he with them? It doesn't make any sense."

"Why don't you ask him?" Garrett said with a wry smile. "And besides, who said it was supposed to make sense?"

"Yeah, I guess so," Dakota muttered sourly. He looked at the broken, bullet-riddled stagecoach, then at the four

17

figures who stood a short distance from the corpse-laden wreck, patiently waiting for their next set of victims. Dakota shook his head gloomily, struck by the iron-fast irreversibility of events, by the utter significance of every choice a person makes. If only he hadn't wakened Garrett, he kept thinking, none of this would have happened. There would still have been an hour or so before they would have broken camp. About now, they probably would have been enjoying a long, leisurely breakfast.

"You know, Garrett," he said, "we're not going to be able to talk ourselves out of this."

"That's for sure," Garrett replied evenly. "After what they did to those people, they're not going to be leaving anyone behind to talk about it." No sooner had he finished pronouncing the words than he thought of the old woman. He looked toward the way station. She was still there, standing near the porch. Motionless, her gaze alternating between Garrett and Dakota and the four men, she seemed as aloof, as impervious to whatever might happen, as ever.

"Well, do you have any ideas?" Dakota was asking. "You've still got the knife, at least. That ought to be worth something."

"That's what I'm counting on," Garrett answered. "Hopefully it'll give us the chance we need. Make sure to keep an eye on me. You'll know when I think the time's come. As soon as I make my move, you go for the one nearest you and try to get his gun. I'll see if I can't do the same. Between us, maybe we'll be able to catch them by surprise."

"Okay," Dakota nodded. "Let's just hope it works."

"One thing's for certain—it's our only chance."

They fell silent and, guiding their horses through the rocks, made the final portion of the descent. At the bottom of the slope, they rode a few paces across the valley floor, reined to a stop, and fixed their attention on the deadly group. The four were lined up side by side, not speaking to one another as they watched the riders' approach. They were each a good thirty years older than Willy, but, like him, were dressed in overalls and faded flannel shirts. And there was another point of similarity between them and their youngest member: each had something the matter with him, was disfigured in some peculiar way. One was missing an arm; another had his jaws set too closely together for him to have had any teeth; the third, bald, with red, bulging eyes, weighed some three hundred pounds; and the last, the most sinister looking of all, had a jagged scar which extended from his right temple, leaving a livid, swollen trail over a closed eyelid and gnarled cheek, down to the side of his chin. Unlike Willy, however, their deformities were far from congenital, but rather had been accumulated in the course of the lives they had led. And this made them all the more menacing. They looked as though they had spent all their years in the wastelands, and, well-suited to their barren surroundings, were as capable of surviving there as the lizard or cactus.

Sizing them up, Garrett stared at the band of grotesques for a long, silent minute before giving Dakota a nod. They lightly spurred their horses and drew closer.

Willy's father, the one with the scar, stepped forward, his pistol drawn.

"All right, get down," he grated.

Neither Garrett nor Dakota made a reply. They knew what value it would have had. As they were dismounting, the bald, hefty man said in a thick voice, pointing to one side, "Hey, look over there. We forgot one."

At the other end of the valley, reeling back and forth as he walked, was the driver of the stagecoach. His clothing tattered and streaked with blood, he was wandering dazedly about, aware only of the pain that shot through his body.

"Go 'n get him, Poole," the scarface said.

"Okay," answered his brutish, oversized companion, and dragged himself off.

Apparently the leader of the group, Willy's father turned and, motioning toward the way station, said to the one-armed man, "And you, Cantrill, bring the hag over here. Might as well have all of 'em together in one place."

Cantrill gave an obliging toss of his head and ambled over to the cabin. Reaching the white-haired woman, he grabbed her by the arm, gave her a quick push toward the others, and snarled, "Git over to 'em, you old witch."

The woman walked slowly, with what seemed almost haughty self-confidence, stumbling every now and again

19

before the other's repeated shoves. Her emaciated features were composed into a rigid, impassive expression.

The toothless man, who had remained behind with Willy's father, had meanwhile drawn his gun and fixed his sights on Garrett and Dakota. "Keep them hands away from yer sides," he said, eyeing them cautiously. He then threw a look over his shoulder and asked, "Should I get their guns, Lavery?"

"Yeah, go ahead," answered the scar-faced leader.

His hollow jaws grinding together in a wary, ruminative motion, the man started toward Garrett. Dakota watched nervously, expectantly, for the sign to be given. Garrett felt his palms moisten as the sunken-featured figure drew closer. There were two six-guns aimed at Dakota and him; this certainly wasn't the best moment to make a move. He didn't want to go for his knife, but couldn't afford to lose it either.

"Hey y' don't have to worry about them. I already got their guns," a voice called.

All heads turned toward the base of the slope, where Willy, on foot, was guiding his horse down from the last of the rocks.

Willy gave a short tug at the bridle and sauntered up to them. He pointed at the holsters dangling from his saddle horn and grinned, "What's the matter, Brady? Y' don't figure I woulda thought of that myself?"

Brady, who was only a few steps from Garrett, and had been about to have a look at what lay beneath the black jacket, spat languidly and shrugged, "Ya coulda forgot, kid. Ya coulda forgot."

"Don't trust me much, do you?" Willy retorted.

"Why should I?" Brady said, a venomous hiss escaping from his empty gums. "We sent you up there t' keep a watch on things. We didn't tell ya nothing 'bout bringin' anyone else into it."

"Hold on, Brady," the elder Lavery cut in, "Willy did right good by stopping 'em. Right good." He then went up to his son, and said, "Okay, boy, tell us what happened."

"I already did," said Willy. "Those two showed up right in the middle of things. I came 'round behind 'em and kept 'em there till it was over so's they wouldn't make any trouble. That's all there is to it."

20

"Mmm ..." Lavery grunted, and rubbed his scarred, stubble-covered face meditatively. He turned to Garrett. "Well, mister, you and the kid here picked a mighty bad time t' turn up."

"Ain't that just what they did," cackled Cantrill, who was standing off to the side with the woman.

Garrett contemplated them with a long, steady look. There were too many guns drawn. The time still wasn't right.

"And what if I said I agreed with you?" he said in a measured tone. "It sure wasn't a good time to turn up. But we didn't plan it that way, you know."

"That may be," answered Lavery. "But now you're here. And there ain't nothin' what's gonna change that."

"And what about when you was up there?" Willy said accusingly. "You saw what was goin' on. If you didn't want no trouble, how come y' didn't just turn around and ride off?"

"We just might have," Garrett replied. "Except you never gave us the chance to."

"Nah, that ain't the way it was," the youth said with a broad, icy smile. "You was fixing on gettin' in on somethin' what wasn't none of yer business. Only I was there to make sure you didn't."

"And what about you, kid?" Brady interrupted. He poked Dakota in the side with his gun barrel. "We ain't heard nothing outta you yet. What d'you got to say?"

Dakota glanced at Garrett. "It's like he told you," he answered quietly. "We weren't going to do anything. It wasn't our fight."

"C'mon, kid," Brady drawled amiably. "Ya sure y'ain't lyin'?" A strange sparkle in his eyes, he dropped his hand on Dakota's shoulder, and, resting it there a moment, gave the flesh beneath the shirt a slight, but unmistakable squeeze.

The harshness of the man's touch, the tentative, yet thoroughly assertive manner in which the fingers groped at his skin, filled Dakota with revulsion. He jerked away.

"What's the matter, kid?" Brady said with another toothless hiss. "What d'ya got to be scared of? I ain't gonna hurt ya none."

Willy and Cantrill began to chuckle. Garrett's face

21

hardened. His arm, stiff with tension, dropped to his hip. But he stopped at the sound of Lavery's voice.

"Okay, okay, that's enough." The scar creased back into a leering smile. "—for now." In answer to the others' disappointed, questioning looks, Lavery threw a glance at Poole, who was then returning with the driver of the stage, and said, "We've got other things to take care of first."

"Sure, Lavery," Brady agreed after a moment's thought. "Fer now."

"Keep an eye on 'em," Lavery said to Cantrill, waving his gun at the prisoners. "You too, Willy." He turned to the approaching figures.

Dakota breathed a sigh of relief. But for Brady, who was standing uncomfortably close, the gruesome band had shifted the focus of their attention.

Poole came trudging toward them at a listless pace. He had an arm wrapped around the neck of the driver and, casually, without the slightest appearance of effort, was dragging the hapless figure along behind him. When he joined the circle, he relaxed the powerful choke hold slightly and drawled, "What d'you want me to do with him now, Lavery?"

"Over this way."

"Okay," Poole droned indifferently. He yanked the driver up from his knees and pulled him the few extra steps that remained between them and the stagecoach.

"Let's go," Cantrill barked. Brandishing his weapon, he shoved each of the captives forward.

Poole let his arm drop from the driver's throat. The dazed, fear-struck man crumpled over with exhaustion.

"Pick him up," said Lavery.

"All right, off the ground." Poole grabbed the driver by the shirt, hauled him to his feet, and pressed him up against the door of the coach.

"What—what do you want from me?" the driver whispered through quivering lips.

"Nothing much," Lavery answered. "Just get up there and throw down the strongbox."

"S-Strongbox?"

"Yeah, you have trouble hearin' or somethin'?" said Poole.

22

"But there isn't any strongbox," the other protested. "We don't carry one on this run."

"Get up there," Lavery warned. "I ain't gonna say it again."

"But there isn't any, I tell you!" The driver turned to the old woman and appealed to her, "Marta, you—you tell them! Maybe they'll believe you."

"No, it is useless. They will not listen," she answered solemnly, in a foreign, heavily inflected accent. "Their ears were not made to hear truth."

"Keep out of this, hag," Lavery snorted. "I'll let you know when I wanna hear something outta you!" He then returned to the driver. "Now let's hear it. You gonna do it or not? I ain't got all day to waste on you."

"But what's the point?" the driver said in a cracking voice. "You think I'm crazy enough to try lying to you? If there was a strongbox up there, I'd—"

The trembling man never got to finish his answer. As he was speaking, Lavery looked at Poole and gave a short nod. Obedient, emotionless, Poole drew his gun and fired. The impact of the bullet sent the driver flying back against the stage. As if the burning lead had nailed him to the side of the coach, he remained on his feet for a last convulsive, life-draining moment, a look of terror frozen to his features. And then he keeled rigidly over, his vitals slowly oozing from the hole in his chest.

The old woman breathed a short, quiet sigh. But her expression did not change: it remained as sober and unflinching as ever.

Brady drew closer to Dakota and chuckled grimly, "Don't worry, kid. Nothin' like that's gonna happen to you." The goatish sparkle reappearing in his eyes, he raised his pistol and began to stroke the youth's cheek with the cold steel of the gun barrel. He murmured reflectively, in a soothing tone which made Dakota's skin crawl, "Nothin' like that at all."

Noticing the look of dark, gnawing anger which was etched into Garrett's features, Cantrill pressed his six-gun into the man's back and growled tauntingly, "You don't like what you see, mister? Maybe you'd like to try to do something about it, huh?"

"No, I don't want to do anything about it," Garrett an-

23

swered coldly. He glanced at Dakota and with his sharp, resolute gaze told the youth to wait patiently, that it would soon be time.

"That's real smart of you, mister." The one-armed man prodded Garrett with another fierce jab of the gun before withdrawing it from his ribs. "Now shut up 'n watch."

"Don't waste yer breath on him, Cantrill," said Lavery. "You know what to do if he gives you any trouble."

Interrupted from his primary concern, Lavery wheeled around to the body of the driver. He dipped his boot into the puddle of gore and, with a contemptuous kick of the heel, rolled the corpse over on its back. He peered intently into the gaping eyes, watched the slow trickle of blood from the twisted, half-parted lips. A smile, the reflection of some morbid inner satisfaction, appeared on Lavery's scarred face.

"Well, that takes care of him," he chortled. "I reckon now we've gotta see to it ourselves."

"Want me to?" asked Poole.

"Naa, that's okay," Lavery answered. He got a foothold on the broken axle and pulled himself up. Atop the coach, he flattened himself across the seat and leaned into the driver's box. His head slowly emerged from the empty compartment. He straightened up and spat disgustedly.

"It looks like he was tellin' the truth, all right," he announced to the others.

"You mean they ain't carryin' no money?" Willy asked.

"Nope, not up here anyways." Lavery's gnarled features twisted into a hopeful smile as he added, "But there's still them other people inside. We oughta find some decent pickin's with them." He swung his legs around the top of the stage and jumped down.

"Now let's see what we've got here." He threw open the door and climbed into the coach.

Five bodies lay strewn across the seats and floor, sprawled on top of one another in rigid silence, like heavy, fully dressed mannequins that had toppled over in shipment. But there was blood, much of it yet undried, seeping from open wounds, making a spreading crimson stain in the bullet-shredded clothing, and here the resemblance ended.

Lavery crawled over the jumbled network of stiffly intertwined limbs and bodies. Finding a space for himself in the cramped, stifling quarters, he got down on all fours, gathered up one of the corpses and shoved it outside. The first body to come tumbling through the open door was that of an aging man dressed in the attire of a successful businessman. He landed with a stony thud on his face, a few feet from the driver. A younger man, also a businessman, was the next to be hurled to the ground. There followed in rapid succession a man and woman, both middle-aged and, quite probably, if the similarities that existed between them could be attributed to years of shared lives, a married couple.

When Lavery came to the last body in the pile—that of a black-haired woman—he allowed himself a pause from his labors. He knelt down beside her on the floor and examined her closely. Unlike the others, her face was not pale and bloodless; she looked as though she were merely asleep. She was in her mid-thirties, but was long past the freshness of her youth. While neither sweet-looking nor pretty, she possessed the kind of dark allure that must have hypnotized many a man who had crossed her path. Bereft of all traces of innocence, her features were strong and aquiline, sharply molded into the shrewd countenance of one who had seen much, done much, in her time. Even in their present immobile state, her prominent jaw and high-ridged cheekbones held fast to the set expression of a woman of strong-willed determination.

Lavery cursed under his breath. It was a pity she was dead. But after brief deliberation he decided with a scornful smile that it wouldn't matter all that much. The only thing missing would be the fight she'd put up.

He reached down, about to run his hand over the well-formed body. At the first instant of his touch, though, he learned that he hadn't studied her closely enough. The eyelids flew open. The lips parted and the tightly held breath, withdrawn to give the appearance of death, came rushing forth in a sharp yell:

"Get off me, you bastard!"

She sprang to her feet and brushed the stunned man aside. She leapt from the coach, into the astonished gazes of the group gathered around the broken vehicle. But she did not get far in her attempted escape. Her jump brought her down on top of one of her fellow passengers. She stumbled over the leaden body and fell to the ground.

Recovering from the surprise a moment before the others, Lavery charged out the door and bounded after her. He landed beside her, quickly got his footing, and grabbed her around the waist.

"Well, well, boys," Lavery said as he hoisted her up and displayed her to his companions, "look what we've got here. One of 'em didn't get shot. The prettiest one, at that. Lucky for us, huh?"

The men stared, openmouthed, feasting their eyes on what stood before them. They missed nothing: the shapely female form, the attractive face, the costly hat that lay in crumpled disarray on the black falling curls, the fashionable dress, now blood-smeared—all was quickly, hungrily, devoured.

"Ain't she somethin'?" Lavery laughed. "A real armful, I tell you. A real armful."

"Let go of me, damn you!" the woman snarled. She swung at him with her arms and tried to squirm free.

Lavery pulled her closer. The tightened hug brought a lustful grimace to his face. "So you were playin' possum with me, were you? What other games d'you like to play?"

"Nothing you'd know how to do," the woman answered with an icy frown.

"Let me have her for a while," Poole said. "We'll see how much fight she's got in her."

"Nah, she ain't right for you," Lavery chuckled. "Heh, you'd break her in half. And I kinda like 'em better when they're in one piece."

"You two can talk about it if you want to," Cantrill suddenly interrupted in a shrill bark. His features were knotted with a fierce tension. "But that ain't fer me. I take what I want." He slapped his pistol into its holster and started for the woman.

Garrett became a little less uneasy. He now had only one gun—Willy's—trained on him. Lavery and his men, occupied with another, more intriguing, matter, had left the task of watching the prisoners to their youngest.

"Give her here!" Cantrill shoved Lavery aside, swung his arm around the woman's head, and pressed her face to his.

She wrenched her lips away in disgust, shouted, "You're gonna be sorry you tried that, pig!" and drove a knee into Cantrill's midsection. Her attacker doubled over.

Garrett restrained a smile. He was getting unexpected help.

Lavery burst into a roaring peal of horselaughter. "What was that, Cantrill? You take what you want?"

"Why you . . ." Cantrill lunged at the woman. He threw himself into her and dragged her to the ground. They rolled and wrestled brutishly, she flailing at him with her arms and legs, he trying to climb atop her and hold her down.

"Forget it, Cantrill," Lavery bellowed. "She's too much for you. Y'need *two* arms for the likes of her."

"Hell, hold still!" Cantrill dug his elbow into the woman's neck and came down on her with the full force of his weight. She sank back, panting for air. The kicking and flailing stopped. Her body became wooden, passive.

"What's the matter?" Cantrill jeered. "Y'ain't fightin' no more." He leaned forward and buried himself in her face.

The woman freed one of her arms. Awkwardly, with a great concentration of effort, she inched it along the ground and reached up, toward her head. Her hand then began to move quickly about, as if groping for something in her hair.

Cantrill's companions laughed and cheered him on. They mistook her strange, fitful movements for those of a woman about to fall into a swoon of passion.

Her hand came to a stop on the hat. It moved back in a slow withdrawing motion, paused for a moment as the fingers gathered into a fist, and then thrust sharply forward and down, into the one-armed man's back.

Cantrill froze. His head and torso rose, arching reflexively away from her. He shut his eyes and let out a long, anguished cry. The woman tugged his elbow from her neck. She drew a gasping breath and pushed him away. Cantrill tumbled from his side onto his back. His screams loudened. He writhed and kicked until his body turned again and fell face-down against the dusty earth. There was a moan, a last twitch, and the writhing ended.

The men looked on in dumbfounded silence, unable to guess what had happened.

In the instant that Cantrill slumped over, Lavery made a sudden instinctive whirl toward the prisoners. "Watch 'em boy! Watch 'em!" he shouted to Willy, and rushed over to the motionless body.

Willy, who had steadily dropped his guard as his interest in the uncanny scene increased, swung around. The Winchester was quickly leveled into position.

Yet Garrett once again felt the urge to smile. The woman had proven herself even more capable than he had guessed. He didn't quite comprehend how, but she had certainly taken care of her end of things. It was now his turn to see to the rest. Calmly awaiting the confrontation he was certain she and Lavery would soon have, he steeled himself into a state of readiness.

As he crouched beside Cantrill, Lavery noticed a small line of blood trickling down the back of the fallen man's shirt. He knelt closer.

"What the ...?" he muttered, scowling. He reached down and removed the long, needle-sharp hatpin that had been driven into Cantrill's spine. He looked at the blood-stained instrument numbly, for the short time it took for everything to sink into place. Bewilderment slowly giving way to seething anger, he rolled the man onto his back. Cantrill stared blankly into the sky, the look of torment etched deeply into his unmoving features.

Garrett caught Dakota's eye and glanced toward Willy's horse, where their holsters were. Dakota gave a slight nod.

Lavery spun from Cantrill to the woman. "You've had it, bitch!" he shouted fiercely. With slow deliberateness, he stood up and raised the silvery needle. The woman scrambled back along the ground.

"You ain't goin' nowhere," Lavery grimaced. "I'm gonna stick this right through you, just like you did to him. 'Cept for you it's gonna take longer, a lot longer." He started toward her.

The muscles in Garrett's face knitted tightly together. Dakota understood what the change of expression meant. He wheeled and ran for the weapons. Simultaneously Garrett threw back the flap of his jacket and pulled the knife from its sheath. He snapped his arm. The gleaming steel ripped through the air.

28

Lavery stopped in mid-stride. The knife had struck squarely. Hilt-deep, it was sunk into the side of his chest. Lavery gaped at the blood rushing from the hole in his body and toppled over.

Dumbstruck, his men watched him fall. Their fate was inscribed and sealed during those few seconds they lost.

The knife had not yet reached its target when Garrett turned and flew at Willy. With one hand, he caught the Winchester by the barrel and yanked it from Willy's grasp. With the other, he threw a tight-fisted punch which sent the youth sprawling backward.

Brady glanced dazedly around. He went for his gun. But before he managed to snap it from the holster, Garrett came at him with the Winchester and with a furious sweep of the weapon slammed the rifle butt into his face. Brady danced back and landed in the dust. And there he remained, a grayish mass of red-tinged gore slowly draining from the break in his skull.

Garrett made a headlong rush at Poole. The hulking man had had sufficient time to draw his gun, but, as sluggish in taking aim as he was with everything else, not enough to fire a shot. The long barrel clenched firmly in his hands, Garrett brought the Winchester down on Poole's shoulder just as the six-gun went off. The pistol fell. The stray bullet kicked up a clod of earth. Garrett raised the rifle and swung out again. Off balance, stumbling back, Poole held up his arms to ward off the blow. The wooden stock struck his thick, powerful wrists and snapped in two. His bulging eyes flashing with fire, he sprang forward. He clamped his hands around Garrett's throat and began to squeeze.

"You don't know it yet, mister," he grunted, "but you're dead."

Garrett dropped the splintered rifle and drove his fists into the other's stomach and chest. But the vigorous blows had no effect. The strangling grip would not loosen.

Poole grinned savagely. "Keep it up if you want to. It ain't gonna help you any. Ain't gonna help you at—"

A crackling burst of gunfire cut him short. The grin dropped from his face. There was a second angry explosion. His fingers opened and released their hold on Garrett. He tried to turn. A third shot rang out, and another

29

piece of hot lead dug its way into his oversized body. He swayed and staggered, trying to keep himself on his feet. A fourth bullet was fired. A sharp, convulsive shudder ran through him; he keeled over and collapsed in a motionless heap.

Calm and resolute, the dark-haired woman lowered the smoking gun. She had taken it from Lavery's holster.

Hers and Garrett's eyes met. They exchanged a smile.

Garrett then threw a glance at Marta, the old woman, to see if she had gotten hurt. The latter, contemplating the corpse-strewn scene with statuesque equanimity, had not moved from her place. Garrett chuckled to himself; nothing seemed to shake her.

He turned next to Dakota, who had taken up a position beside Willy's horse. He was holding Garrett's carbine.

"I'm sorry, Garrett," the youth called. "I couldn't get off a shot. You were in my line of fire."

"That's okay," Garrett replied. "It worked out all right just the same." His gaze moved to the body lying at his feet. Noticing the four closely spaced holes in Poole's back, he said to the younger of the two women, "You know, that was pretty good shooting."

"No, it wasn't," she answered. "One bullet should've been enough to bring him down."

As were the other three, she was unaware of the crawling figure coming up behind her.

Barely alive, his side open, streaming red, Lavery slithered toward her. He reached out, caught her by the ankle, and jerked her to the ground. Clutching her leg, he dragged himself closer. His arm rose.

The first to see the hatpin Lavery was holding, about to sink it into the prostrate woman's back, Garrett scrambled toward him.

"Stay back!" Dakota shouted. He swung the carbine to his shoulder and took aim.

In mid-stride, still a few bounding paces from Lavery, Garrett looked in the direction of the youth. He swerved and stopped short an instant before the thundering *crack!* sounded.

Knocked unconscious by Garrett's first punch, Willy came to in time to see the bullet tear into his father's body, to hear the anguished moan as his father slumped

30

back into a pool of blood. Willy trembled; his misshapen features were filled with horror and confusion. The head moved from side to side. The bird-eye darted about, incredulously taking in the corpses of Brady, Cantrill and Poole.

Disbelief turned into all-consuming terror as Willy sprang to his feet and made a dash for his companions' horses.

Glimpsing the running figure out of the corner of his eye, Dakota shifted his stance and fired the carbine a second time.

The bullet caught Willy in the back of the leg. He fell to his knees, but hurriedly gathered himself up and hobbled to the nearest horse. As he pulled his weight into the saddle, he peered over his shoulder, at Dakota. The fear and powerlessness dissolved into a look of bitter, fiery hatred.

The two youths, equal in years, their roles reversed, regarded each other in silence for a brief, time-suspended moment.

A sudden chill ran through Dakota. He lowered the carbine. Struck by something out of his past, something that leapt into his mind from the dark realm of memory, he watched passively as Willy slapped the reins and galloped off into the hills.

When the lone rider dropped behind the barren ridge the stagecoach and four horsemen had descended a short while earlier, Dakota sighed and lowered his eyes. He tucked the carbine under his arm and started back to the others.

Two

The Blood of the Dead

The windows, few and small, brought only the faintest traces of light into the cabin. The low ceiling threw a shroud of murky shadow over the room. Pauses in conversation produced a raw hush which heightened the gloom and made it all the more pervasive. Random, fleeting sounds would rush in to fill the void of silence and become unnervingly sharp. The short gusts of the wind outside, the flames dancing and crackling in the hearth, the footfalls coming from behind the closed door of an adjoining room, the creaking of a chair—the noises weighed in from all sides, imposing their presence on the oppressive stillness.

The old woman removed a pot from the fire, tilted back the lid and peered in. "Ah, it is ready," she said, and shuffled across the room to Garrett and Dakota, who were seated at the end of a crude wooden table lined on either side by long benches.

Garrett raised his metal cup to her and she poured out the steaming coffee. "And what about you?" Marta said, turning to Dakota. "What would you like? I am sorry, I should have asked you before."

"The coffee will be fine," replied the youth.

"Oh, you drink it? Good, good . . ."

"It is strange," she added in a reflective tone while filling his cup, "but it was not until I was some years older than you that my parents allowed me my first drink of coffee."

"Why was that?" Dakota asked. "There's nothing wrong with it."

"It was one of the customs of my land, nothing more,"

32

she replied. "I do not know if it was the same in the homes of your country, but even so, it does not matter. That was a long time ago. Much has changed since then. Customs vanish as rapidly as the seasons."

"Now that you bring it up," Garrett put in, "would you mind if I asked where you come from?"

"The name is of little importance. Few people have ever heard of it before. It is a place very far from here." Marta smiled and set the pot and cloth holder down between the two seated figures. She then went back to her rocking chair beside the hearth, took up a long wooden spoon, and began to stir the contents of the large kettle that hung over the fire.

Another brief, yet seemingly interminable, silence reigned. It was broken by the clicking of a latch.

The door to the next room opened, and the dark-haired woman, now dressed in a white blouse which was tucked into a pair of tight-fitting denim jeans, appeared in the threshold. She leaned a large tan carpetbag against the wall and strode up to the table.

Marta contemplated her with a mixture of curiosity and disapproval. *Yes,* she thought as she rocked back and forth in her chair, *much indeed has changed*.

"Well, that sure's a different outfit all right," Garrett noted with a chuckle.

"What's the matter?" said the woman. "Don't you like it?"

"No, no, I like it fine. Better than the first, as a matter of fact."

"I thought it would be an improvement," she responded drily. "Not that that's saying much. The bloodstains didn't do much for the other one."

"Oh, yes—your dress," Marta interrupted quickly, as though she had just remembered something of grave importance. "Where is it?"

"I put it in there," the second woman answered with surprise, pointing at the carpetbag. "Why?"

"You are not thinking of wearing it again, are you?" Marta asked worriedly.

"Not before I've given it a good washing."

"And then you will wear it?"

"Sure. If it's not been ruined."

Marta lowered her eyes and murmured in a mournful tone, "Ah, that is not a good idea. Not a good idea at all."

"Why, is there something else I should do with it?" the woman asked, faintly amused.

"Yes, yes, there is," Marta pronounced solemnly. "You must burn it. Burn it until the last shred is consumed, until only ashes remain. In this manner alone can the blood of the dead be purged. You are wrong to believe that it can simply be washed away."

The others regarded her with various degrees of bewilderment. Illuminated by the rays of firelight, her emaciated features were bathed in a pale, flickering glow. It lent her a spectral appearance, a presence as odd and striking as her strange accent.

"It is important you do this," she continued. "For otherwise you may bring much ill fortune upon yourself."

"Well, I'll give it some thought," the younger woman said.

Marta breathed a heavy sigh. "I can see you do not take me seriously. I am sorry. It is a pity you cannot accept my advice."

The woman smiled. "Was it advice or a warning?"

"There is rarely a difference between the two," Marta replied. "They are, as your fellow countrymen say, opposite sides of the same coin."

"Well, whatever you call it, it's pretty hard to do something just because someone tells you to. Especially if you don't see any reason for it."

"Yes, I know. I have seen it all too often. People do not listen." Marta then added, her voice more solemn than ever, "But let me tell you, there are many things which are beyond comprehension. Among them are the omens, the portents of evil. And when they are seen, they should be heeded."

Her gaze, narrow and piercing, roamed across the faces of her guests. She shook her head ruefully and got up from the chair.

"Enough," she sighed. "There is nothing more to be said." Waving the woman toward the third setting at the table, Marta softly told her, "Why don't you sit down and join the others in some coffee. The meal will soon be ready."

Marta turned, picked up the spoon, and dipped it into the kettle.

Shifting her eyes away from Marta, the dark-haired woman glanced at Garrett and Dakota. They both answered her with equally bewildered expressions. The three shot another look across the cabin. Their stares lingered thoughtfully on the shrunken, timeworn figure stooped over the fire.

"Here," Garrett said, and pushed back the bench. The woman nodded distractedly and sat down beside him.

Dakota wrapped the cloth around the handle and lifted the coffeepot. "Would you like some?" he asked.

"Yes, I would." She reached for the coffee.

"That's all right," said Dakota. "I'll pour it." He stood up and leaned across the table.

Watching the dark, seething liquid rise in her cup, Dakota found himself remembering the fight she'd had with Cantrill. He thought of how she had looked, pinned to the ground, her skirts upraised, the exposed legs frenziedly thrashing at the one-armed man. Dakota's blood stirred; a thrill of excitement ran through him. The turbulent sensation which had first caught him in its feverish grip in the early years of youth, and had become more insistent and confusing with each new stage of awakening desire, once again began to gnaw at him.

"There you are," he said quietly, with reserve. He put down the pot and sank back onto the bench.

The woman thanked him and flashed a warm, pleasant smile which made Dakota's heart pound all the more furiously. But after stealing a few admiring glances at her, he felt a change come over him. The reality of her presence impressed itself upon him, breaking the spell of his fantasies. The wild, voluptuous images dissolved, and were replaced by a surge of shame and guilt.

"Sure tastes good," the woman murmured with her first sip of the warming brew.

"Nothing better on a day like this," Dakota replied, managing to maintain a semblance of outward calm while the struggle against emotions he could neither control nor understand pressed on within.

"I don't know about that," she said. "I think I could come up with a couple of things which might be a little better. Some good bourbon, for one. Not too much, mind you. Just enough to turn the trick, and that would be fine."

Garrett smiled. "It's a little early for that, isn't it?"

"Well, I guess it's all a matter of how you look at things," she answered. "You might call it early, but as far as I'm concerned this day's lasted too long already."

"I know what you mean," Garrett chuckled. "It sure hasn't been much of a morning, has it?"

"No, it sure hasn't."

Dakota contemplated them vacantly. He wrenched himself free of his thoughts and, reassembling the words he had just heard spoken, realized that it wasn't the weather they were discussing.

"It could have been worse," he ventured. "At least we came out of it in one piece."

"Maybe," the woman said, "but we had a lot of luck going for us. I wouldn't want to see if it would work again. You know, it can only be pushed so—" She stopped abruptly and turned.

Hurriedly coming up to the table, Marta bent over her and asked, "Tell me, what is your name?"

"What?" the woman retorted in surprise.

"Please, tell me your name," Marta repeated anxiously. "It is important that I know it."

"Layla Magnum. Why?"

Marta repeated the name to herself in a whisper, then said aloud, "Good, good. It may be of help."

As puzzled by her now as they had been a few minutes before, the others watched her shuffle back across the room to the hearth. Once again, she reached for the spoon and attended to the meal. But they could see that her mind was elsewhere. She was peering intently into the fire. Her lips were moving in the rapid, indistinct undertone of prayer. They caught a word or two of what she said, enough to realize that it was not meant for their ears. She was speaking in a foreign—most likely her native— tongue.

A long pause followed. The low, rhythmic murmur of Marta's incantations filled the darkened room.

From outside there came another prolonged, whistling

gust, and Layla remarked quietly, merely to break the heavy silence, "It sounds like the wind's picking up."

"It's been the same the past three or four days," Garrett noted. "It just keeps blowing like that without letting up."

"There's going to be a storm," said Dakota. "A bad one."

"You said that yesterday," Garrett smiled. "And the day before that, if I remember right."

"It's coming," the youth replied in a confident tone. "Those clouds are getting bigger and darker all the time. We'll be in for it pretty soon."

"Well, if it could hold out for another day or so, it'd sure be fine with me," Layla mused.

Garrett nodded. "Same here."

The conversation, made up of casual observations which rang hollowly against the stillness of the cabin, continued a short while longer, a means of idling away the time until Marta began serving the meal.

Her mysterious pronouncements over the fire completed, the aged woman emerged from her trancelike state a good deal more at ease than before. Acting as though nothing out of the ordinary had taken place, she set the kettle down on the edge of the table, took her guests' plates and gave them each a generous serving of lamb stew. She then removed the kettle and brought back in its place a basket of bread she had been warming by the hearth.

"Please eat," she told them with a polite, agreeable smile. "I hope you will enjoy it."

"Aren't you going to have any?" Garrett asked.

"No, no, do not worry about me," Marta said. "I do not take my meal until much later in the day."

Garrett's brow narrowed quizzically. He said after a moment's pause, "Could you answer one thing for me?"

"Why, of course," Marta replied pleasantly. "If I am able. What is it?"

"Who were you making this for if it wasn't for you? It must have been cooking a good couple of hours before any of us happened by this way."

From her previous actions and comments, Garrett expected Marta to answer that she had known of their coming, that this as well as the morning's many other chance occurrences had all been foretold, but she said instead:

"It is not as curious a matter as you may think. I had prepared this meal yesterday afternoon, for the people on the stagecoach. They were due to arrive here before evening, but, as you yourself saw, they did not come until just before—"

"We were delayed slightly," Layla interrupted, an ironic edge to her voice. "We had to make an unexpected stop."

Garrett turned to her. "Why? What happened?"

"There was a sixth passenger with us on the stage when we started out two days back. This one you wouldn't have any way of knowing about; she didn't make it as far as the rest of us. She was a real pretty thing—couldn't have been much more than seventeen or eighteen. A young girl, but still old enough to know how to land herself in a mess of trouble. And she was sure in trouble, all right. About six months' worth, from the way she looked when we finally found out why she was so sick."

"You mean she was with child, yes?" Marta asked.

"That's one way of putting it," Layla said. She took another sip of coffee and then continued, "I'll tell you, though, she was pretty good at keeping it a secret. None of us could see that anything was the matter—not at first anyway. And the same probably went for the people who run the stage, because you can bet they wouldn't have sold her a ticket if they'd known. But no one knew, which I guess is just how she wanted it. I can't think of any other reason why she would have had herself all strapped up the way she was.

"The first day out, like I said, we didn't notice anything. She was a little quiet, but the rest of us weren't doing all that much talking either. It was a rough, uncomfortable ride, worse than most stages I've been on. We were a little behind schedule and the driver was trying to make up for lost time, so we were going faster than usual. I can't imagine what all that bouncing around must have done to her, but she didn't let it show until the next day—yesterday—when it was already too late. She became sick after breakfast, and later, in the stage, when we could see that she was getting weaker and weaker, she kept telling us that there was no need to stop, that she was sure she'd be feeling better soon.

"By noon she was so bad off we gave up listening to her. The men went out to start up a fire, giving me and the other woman with us a chance to have a look at her. That's when we found that contraption she'd rigged up for keeping the world from knowing her secret. It might have been good for that, but not for much else. The damn thing was worse than a corset. And she'd been wearing it too tightly for too long. I don't think there's a doctor anywhere who could have helped her at that time."

She paused reflectively before adding, "We sure couldn't."

"There must be whole lot easier ways to go," Garrett muttered grimly.

"I suppose so," Layla said with a short nod, "but hers certainly wasn't one of them. It took a long, long time, and with more pain than I've ever seen a person go through. The end didn't come till nightfall. By then it was the best thing that could've happened to her."

"Why did she do it?" Dakota asked. "I mean, try to make a trip like that. Didn't she know what it would do to her?"

"Who knows what was going through her mind," Layla sighed. "But if I had to make a guess, I'd say it probably had something to do with the man who'd gotten her that way in the first place."

"You think she was trying to find him?" the youth said.

"Or running away from him," Layla answered with a smile. "There's nothing saying it couldn't have been the other way around. He might have loved her, might even have wanted to marry her, while she didn't want to have any part of it. You don't hear about it as often, but it's been known to happen every once in a while. It's not always the man who's looking for ways to get out of marriage, you know. Some women like to keep their freedom too."

A look of perplexity appeared on Marta's wizened features. Such ideas were new to her.

"I am not certain I can agree with you," she said after pondering the matter. "A woman does not have thoughts of that kind when she is with child."

39

"Maybe, maybe not," Layla replied in an easy tone. "I've known a few who were in the same boat as that girl."

"Yes?" Marta said with curiosity. "And what did they do?"

"Well, some did one thing, some did another. Everybody's got their own way of working out their problems."

A hint of sadness in her smile, Layla gave a shrug of her shoulders. There was little else to say on the subject.

The meal was long and leisurely; the conversation rambled pleasantly from topic to topic. When her guests had finished their first serving, Marta came over with the blackened kettle and filled their plates with another helping of stew. An hour later, after all appetites had been more than satisfied, she cleared away the dishes, returned with a fresh pot of coffee and an extra cup for herself, and joined them at the table. As they sat together and talked on, relaxing over their drinks, a gradual, barely perceptible change came over the room. The oppressive stillness no longer reigned; the aura of gloom began to recede.

"You run this place all by yourself?" Garrett asked, glancing about the cabin.

"Yes, that is right," said Marta.

"What ever brought you to these parts? You're a long way from home, aren't you?"

"I have been living here for many years," Marta replied. "Just why I chose to do so would be difficult to explain—to myself as well as to you. Decisions are often made without our knowledge of the why or how. We simply do certain things without questioning ourselves. Something tells us that we should, that it would be best for us, and we do it. What of you? Have you not occasionally made decisions you were unable to account for?"

Garrett smiled. "A few." For an instant his gaze came to rest on Dakota.

"There are seldom more than a few, but they are an important few just the same," Marta said in a quiet, measured voice. "They are the choices which change our lives the most, which take us, as you just said, further and further from home."

"Doesn't it get kind of lonely out here for you?" Dakota asked.

"No, not at all," said Marta. "Many people stop here to rest from their journey. And, like the three of you, they are most interesting to speak with. For some reason they act differently here than they do when they are home among friends. Perhaps it is because they are so far from everyone and everything they know, perhaps it is because I am a stranger to them, but with me they speak freely, openly. They find themselves telling me things which have long been on their minds, things which they have never told anyone else."

"Like what, for instance?"

With a smile of confident wisdom, Marta answered the youth, "Every subject you can imagine has probably been discussed here at one time or another. Travelers always have stories to relate—" with this she glanced at Layla, "—about themselves, about others. And in these stories they reveal much of themselves, much indeed. One merely has to sit back and listen."

"I bet you can learn a lot about a person like that," Layla said, giving her a meaningful look.

"Yes, at times."

"I can imagine." Layla thought a moment about her narrative of the previous day's events, and then said, taking the conversation in another direction, "While we're on the subject of traveling, I've still got some to do myself. Have you heard of a town called New Eden? That's where I'm headed."

"New Eden?" replied Marta. "Yes, I know of it. Some of the stagecoaches make their next stop there. But not very many, I am afraid. If I am not mistaken, there is only one a week which goes to New Eden. Yours was to go there, was it not?"

"Yes. Except that one's not going anywhere anymore."

Marta nodded grimly. "It will then be another week before the next one arrives. I know it will be an inconvenience for you, but if you wish to wait—"

"Well, I had something else in mind," Layla said. "I noticed you had some horses outside. Would you be able to spare one of them?"

"You are able to ride a horse?"

"Of course," Layla said, amused at the other's surprise. "I'm not dressed in this getup for nothing."

"Oh, I had not thought—"

"Is there something so strange about a woman riding horseback?"

"No, no, it is just that I have seen few who do."

"Well, all I need is a saddle to go with one of those horses out there and you'll be able to see it again."

"Certainly; it will not be any trouble. You may have what you wish," answered the old woman.

"Good. Then that only leaves me with the problem of how to get there."

"It should not be difficult for you," said Marta. "If you travel directly eastward, it will be the first town you reach."

"That sounds easy enough. Is it far?"

"I have not been there myself, but I understand that it is not far at all. It is on the other side of the Texas border, only three or four hours from here."

"We're that close to Texas?" Garrett broke in. "I figured it was still a good day's ride from here."

"No," said Marta, "it is much nearer than that. It is merely a few miles to the border."

Garrett turned to Dakota. "Hmm, I guess we've made more progress than we thought."

"Why? Where in Texas are you going?" Layla asked.

"Nowhere in particular," Garrett replied. "We just thought we'd come down this way to see what there is to see."

Layla smiled. "Sounds like a familiar way of doing things."

"What about you? What brings you this way?"

"Oh, pretty much the same thing."

"But why New Eden? It sounds to me like it's a pretty small town. How'd you ever come to pick that one?"

"Simple. I've got a job waiting for me there. That's enough for me to be willing to give the place a try."

"Can't argue with that."

Garrett was about to ask her what kind of work she

42

did, but, on an impulse, decided against it. He had the feeling he already knew what the answer would be.

"Listen, we're going in that direction anyway," he found himself saying instead. "How'd you like some company?"

"Well, I can't see why not. As a matter of fact, it would probably be a good idea if you did. I'm not much good at finding places. The two of you might be able to keep me from getting lost."

"Fine," Garrett said, returning her smile. He then asked Dakota, "Is that all right with you?"

Dakota took his eyes off the dark-haired woman long enough to make his reply.

"Sure."

Three

The Buried
and Unburied

The door creaked open. They filed out of the cabin and crossed the porch. One after the next, they stopped and peered thoughtfully into the center of the valley. Temporarily set aside in their minds, purposely left unspoken, the morning's events came rushing forward in a horde of bleak memories. Though spared another glimpse of the grisly array of corpses—upon Marta's suggestion they had placed the passengers and their assailants inside the stagecoach before going in to eat—they were provided with other grim reminders of the violent encounter. The large, formless patches of dried blood that stained the dusty earth; the wrecked stage which, fit for little else, now served as a desolate wooden tomb for murderers and victims alike; the pistols and rifles that were scattered across the landscape—each of the four found something to dwell upon.

The first to dispel the lingering images, Garrett quietly said, "Well, I guess we'd better get them buried."

"No, that should not be of concern to you," Marta said. "You have a journey before you. I will see to them."

"Do you have any idea how much work that is?" Garrett replied. "You can't do it by yourself."

"There is no need for you to worry. I will manage, believe me."

The others exchanged a look. With a baffled toss of their heads, they left the matter at that.

The topic already forgotten as far as she was con-

44

cerned, Marta caught hold of the railing to support her time-withered frame and slowly shuffled down from the porch. She turned and told Layla, "Come and look at the horses. Then you may make your selection."

"What about those?" Dakota asked. He pointed at the horses that had belonged to Lavery's men. Gathered earlier, they were tied up alongside the stage. "They're all saddled up and everything. And their owners sure aren't going to miss them any."

"Oh, I'd forgotten about them," Layla murmured abstractedly. There was a tentative note in her voice as she asked the aged woman, "Would you mind if I took one of yours instead?"

"No, I do not mind," Marta said with a sympathetic smile. "Come along, come along."

They walked around the side of the cabin, to the corral. Layla went up to the fence and leaned against the railing. Dakota climbed up on a rung beside her, and together they looked over the horses.

"I like the roan," Layla said, not taking long to single out what seemed to her the likeliest mount.

"That's the one I would have picked," Dakota agreed, smiling broadly.

Behind the cabin was a small stable, where Garrett found the requisite gear. He threw an old and worn saddle—the best he could find—over his shoulder, took a bridle from one of the racks, and went into the corral. The roan responded to his approach with docility, even a touch of friendliness, and he had little trouble getting it equipped.

When he came through the gate, leading the roan by the reins, Garrett said, "You made a good choice. She shouldn't give you any trouble at all."

"I guess I should have looked a little closer," Layla drily replied. "If I'd known it was a *she* I might have picked a different one. I don't usually get along too well with other women."

She came up beside the mare and, stroking it affectionately, said, "Well, honey, it looks like it's you and me now. I hope you won't mind too much."

The horse answered her with a contented whinny.

"What do you know," Layla laughed, "maybe we'll be good friends after all."

She took the reins from Garrett. Dakota swung the gate closed. The four returned to the front of the cabin.

Layla hitched the mare to the corner porch post, alongside Garrett and Dakota's mounts. She then went to get her carpetbag, which she had left inside the cabin. Emerging from the doorway a moment later, she put down the bag, opened it, and produced a beaded drawstring purse.

"How much do I owe you?" she asked Marta.

The aged woman appeared somewhat surprised by the question. "You do not owe me anything," she replied.

"Of course I do. The horse—"

"I do not wish for you to pay me for it," Marta quietly answered. "If circumstances were otherwise, perhaps I would. But you are taking it only because you have no other alternative."

"I don't see where that matters any. I'm taking it just the same. So I think I ought to give you something for it."

"No, that is not necessary," Marta said, waving the purse aside. "Consider it a loan if you wish. When you no longer need the horse you may return it to me."

"But there won't be any way for me to do that," Layla replied. "I'm not planning to be coming back this way."

"Do not worry about your plans," Marta said with a gentle smile. "They are often altered. Life always finds a way of offering the unexpected."

Layla eyed the old woman mistrustfully. "You sound like you know something I don't."

The smile broadened. "No, I assure you, I do not. It is merely a feeling—" She glanced at Garrett and Dakota, meaning to include them as well, "—but I think we all will see one another again."

"Well, time will tell if you're right," said Garrett.

"Yes," Marta agreed with a slow nod, "time will tell."

"Then you're sure you don't want me to give you anything for the horse?" Layla asked. She was pushing the point further than she normally would have. But there was something about Marta—her seeming certainty about matters regarding which she should have had no certainty—which brought out the contrariness in Layla.

"I am quite sure," Marta nodded. "Take the horse."

46

"All right, that's one thing," Layla persisted, "but what about the meal? You'll at least let me pay for that, won't you?"

"Please, you were my guests. I invited you to eat with me. If you enjoyed what you had, that would be payment enough."

Layla smiled and yielded before Marta's graciousness. "Well, you sure don't have to worry about that," she said while slipping the purse back into her carpetbag. "I certainly did."

When Garrett and Dakota echoed her sentiments, Marta said, her wizened features beaming warmly, "Thank you. I am glad you all were so pleased with it."

"I still think you've got it reversed," Layla remarked. "It's we who should be thanking you. Hospitality like yours isn't all that easy to come by."

But Marta, who came from a different world, a different time, could not see it that way. For her, politeness was to be pursued as a matter of course, to be granted everyone as a matter of common decency. But never, as a matter of pride, to be acknowledged.

"There is no comparison," she insisted. "You have given me much more to be grateful for. Very much more."

She turned her gaze in the direction of the stagecoach.

A solitary gust of wind punctuated a thoughtful silence.

"The way I see it," said Layla, "we *all* can be grateful for the way that turned out."

"Yeah, I guess so," Garrett muttered, he, like the others, briefly turning over in his mind the details of the fight. He broke off his reflections when he found himself considering the various things which could have gone wrong and ended all in blackness. He said in a subdued voice, "Well, we'd better be going."

There was another gust of wind. Dakota glanced at the gathering clouds. "I think that's a good idea," he said.

A grin, wry and slightly weary, appeared on Garrett's face. "You're still waiting for that storm, aren't you, boy?"

"No," Dakota replied, "just hoping to avoid it if it does happen to come this way."

"You've got company there," said Layla. She picked up

the carpetbag and followed Garrett and Dakota to the horses.

Marta remained on the porch, her attention centered on the bag, which Layla raised to her shoulders and hung from the saddle horn. Her thoughts elsewhere, Marta watched as they undid the reins and mounted. Suddenly, having come to some decision, she stepped down and went over to Layla.

"Please remember to think about what I told you," she advised in a confidential tone. "It would be best if you did not wear that dress again."

Layla looked at her with surprise and curiosity. "That's really on your mind, isn't it?" she replied.

"I only wish what is best for you. I would not have mentioned it a second time otherwise."

"Well, I appreciate that. But I still can't see why I shouldn't."

"For the same reason you did not want those men's horses," Marta said. "And you were wise to feel that way. They are the property of the dead, and with the dead they should remain."

"But that and the dress are two different things."

"No, they are the same," the other pronounced solemnly. "Very much the same."

Sighing, Layla responded, "Well, I guess we just don't agree."

"I know, I know. Our beliefs are quite different."

The aged woman's features softened. "In spite of that," she added with a faint smile, "I hope you do not mind that I said those few words for you before."

"What do you mean?"

"Inside, when I asked you your name," Marta explained. "Perhaps I should have told you why——"

"No, that's all right," Layla laughed. "I can't say I understood a word of it, but I kind of guessed that was what you were doing."

"Then you do not mind. Good, good . . ."

"But it would be a lot better if I got rid of that dress, right?"

"Yes, it would. But there is nothing more I can say. You must make your own decision." Her gaze lingered on

48

Layla a moment longer and then moved to Garrett and Dakota.

"And now I will let you go on your way," she said. "I have kept you long enough."

The leavetakings were brief, yet marked by warmth and mutual respect. With a few additional words of gratitude for the meal, for the horse, the three riders slapped the reins and slowly moved off.

As they passed the stagecoach each of them cast a last meditative look at the wreckage. Repelled by the air of death which seemed to surround that part of the valley, they rode on at a quickened pace.

"I wonder why she didn't want us to help her bury them," Dakota said. "That's a big job—more than she can handle."

Layla, who was riding between the other two, shook her head. "You've got me there. But for that matter, there are a lot of things about her I can't figure."

Garrett glanced back over his shoulder. Her distance-shrunken figure as statuelike as it had been when he first saw her, Marta was standing before the cabin, watching their departure.

Garrett shifted around in the saddle. "Yeah, she's really something, isn't she."

"About as superstitious as they come," Layla replied.

Dakota's eyes narrowed thoughtfully. As Garrett had done a moment earlier, he threw a last look back. The question that had been gathering in his mind for most of the morning began to take shape. But he hesitated, uncertain whether, given audible form, it could be understood.

"Remember the one from that gang, the one who was missing an arm?" he finally said. "He called her a witch."

Garrett looked at him. "What about it?"

"Well . . . do you think she really is one?"

"A witch?" responded Garrett. "Come on, that doesn't sound like you."

"No, wait a minute. That's not what I meant. I'm not saying I believe in those kinds of things. But what about her? What if *she* does? Isn't that in a way enough to make her one? If a person believes hard enough in something, that's all that counts, isn't it? In the end he could become

49

that something, and it wouldn't make any difference what anyone else thinks."

"So she's become a witch because she believes she *can* become one?" said Layla.

"Yes, in a way . . ."

Garrett and Layla smiled. The youth's logic was not unassailable, perhaps, but his point was worth considering.

"I don't know if I'm right one way or the other," Dakota continued. "But at least it's one way of explaining the way she acted and all. And as far as that goes, it doesn't matter how you explain it, it's still pretty strange."

"Strange enough," Layla nodded. "Just like everything else that's happened today."

They skirted around a group of hills which had risen before them. The way station dropped from view.

The weariness with which Layla had made her last comment reminded Garrett of something. "By the way, I was meaning to ask you," he said, "how was it that you were the only one on the stage who didn't get hurt?"

"I guess I was plain lucky," she answered with a shrug. "When we were coming down the hill we hit a rock or something and I was thrown to the floor. I must have been knocked unconscious, because the next thing I knew all the shooting had stopped and I was just lying there with all of those bodies on top of me. I was trying to get out from under the pile when—well, you know what happened after that. The rest of my luck I owe to both of you."

"I wouldn't say that," Garrett smiled. "You did your part."

"That's right," said Dakota, "you gave us the chance we needed."

"Okay, okay," Layla conceded, "then we all did our share."

They laughed and rode on.

"You know, it's a funny thing," Layla added. "But after all we've been through together, you'd think we'd at least know each others' names."

"Well, we know yours," Garrett replied. "You yourself told us. Just before we ate."

"Oh, that's right, I almost forgot. So I guess that leaves me at a disadvantage."

Garrett leaned forward and, looking past her, said to Dakota, "We can always fix that, can't we?"

"It shouldn't be too much trouble," the youth smiled, and the introductions began.

"Garrett ... Dakota ..." Layla said, nodding to each of them. "Are you father and son?"

"No," answered Dakota, "we just ride together."

"Well, from the way the two of you handled yourselves before, I'd say you make a pretty good team."

Dakota was about to remark that she hadn't done so badly herself, when the sudden sting of memory, of conscience, stopped the words from reaching his lips. He recognized the feeling that prevented him from treating the subject lightly. It was the same chill of regret which the sight of Willy, alone and desperate, hobbling to the horses, had produced in him, the same numbing of the senses which had forced him to lower his carbine and allow the other youth's escape.

His perceptions recoiling inward, Dakota rode along beside Garrett and Layla in silence. He could hear their conversation, but it seemed muffled and remote, and reached him only in meaningless fragments.

His gaze wandered; the introspective search pressed on. He wrestled with his guilt, tried to understand its source. He thought back to what had taken place only a few hours earlier and sifted through the strange series of events, searching for meanings. He and Garrett breaking camp. The gunfire which led them to the way station. The stagecoach. The passengers. The gunmen. The many deaths. The death of one man in particular, the man he, Dakota, had killed: Lavery. Willy's father.

Recalling the look of hatred which Willy had directed at him before riding off, Dakota realized that he, too, had once felt that bitterness, that impotent rage. Six years ago. The day five horse thieves had descended upon his family's ranch and murdered his parents.

The images ceased spinning through his mind. Everything suddenly fell into place.

In the brief moment when his and Willy's eyes met, he now understood, he had seen the similarity between himself and the horse thieves of his past. From Willy's standpoint—which, fleetingly, had become his own as well—he was a murderer and little else. And in the instant when the escape could have been prevented he had exchanged places with the second youth, had once again experienced the painful desolation of being orphaned. It was for this reason that he had been unable to pull the trigger. To have killed Willy then would have been like killing a part of himself. In a way he could not explain, they had merged into one, had become markedly different aspects of a complex whole. He *couldn't* have shot Willy. They had seemed too much alike. . . .

The distant thunder of rifle fire interrupted Dakota's reflections. Coming from somewhere behind him, four evenly spaced reports rang out.

The three riders snapped around. They saw a billowing cloud of smoke rising from the land.

"What is it?" asked Layla.

"Whatever it is," Garrett said, "it's not coming from far off." He glanced at a nearby row of hills. "If we get up there we should be able to see what's going on."

They turned from their course and made their way up the rocky grade. When they reached the higher vantage point, they peered across the desolate stretches and sighted the way station—and then the source of smoke. Standing a short distance from the cabin was a solitary, antlike figure which, like them, was watching as something in the center of the valley went up in flames.

"The stagecoach?" Dakota said in puzzlement.

"That's what it is, all right," Garrett nodded. "She must have been planning to do that all along. That's why she told us she'd be able to manage without our help."

"Well, I guess it's a lot easier than burying them," Layla said.

"But what about those shots?" Dakota asked. "What were they for?"

After a reflective pause, Layla said, "I think I can answer that one. There were four shots, right?"

"Yes . . ."

"And those men's horses—the ones you asked me if I wanted—weren't there four of them as well?"

"You think she killed them?"

"What was it she said?" Layla smiled in response.

52

"Whatever belongs to the dead should remain with the dead?"

They threw a last look at Marta's unmoving form, at the flaming pyre, then descended the hill and continued eastward.

The terrain changed gradually. Stunted plant growth, the first feeble signs of life, began to emerge from the barrenness. The massive formations of stone became fewer and smaller, giving way to rolling plains. The arid landscape slowly receded into the distance, and was replaced by vast expanses of windswept grass.

It was already well into the afternoon when the three travelers reached the crest of a broad ridge and reined to a stop. Below, a mile or two away, there stood a small town. Surrounded by sprawling Texas rangelands that stretched off as far as the eye could see, it seemed—like the way station—isolated, forgotten.

"Do you think that's New Eden?" said Dakota.

"Well, there's only one way to find out," Layla replied.

As they started down the slope, Layla looked up at the sky and, noticing that the clouds were less dark and ominous than before, she remarked, "I guess you were wrong about that storm. It doesn't look like we're going to be in for it after all."

"That's fine with me," said Dakota. "I can do without it easy enough."

Despite its appearance from a distance, it was a thriving community. The settlers of the town had known what they were doing when they brought their Conestogas to a halt at the bottom of the valley. For miles around there were large ranches, and anyone enterprising enough would certainly be able to make a living off the cattlemen's needs.

The main street was lined with shops of all kinds; the remaining areas were filled with long rows of small, cozy homes. The people who had come here from the East with hopes of setting up businesses of their own had little reason for complaint. The passing years had brought prosperity. A pleasant and peaceful setting in which to live and work, it was the town of their dreams.

The three wanderers were approaching a group of old-timers who were seated on benches in front of the livery stable, when Garrett said, "Let's ask them."

"There's no need to," Layla responded. "We're in the right place." Her gaze was fixed on a point further down the street.

She rode on, leading them in the direction of a large white building whose grandly styled facade made a striking contrast with the adjacent lines of shops. Over its porch hung two signs, on which were printed in identical lettering, bold and red:

SCARLET PALACE HOTEL
SCARLET PALACE SALOON

"Well, here we are," Layla said, and dismounted. "Would you like to come in?"

"Sure, why not," Garrett answered. "We could use a place to rest up."

Layla tied her roan to the hitching rail, lifted her carpetbag from the saddle horn, and strode up to the porch. There were two entrances. With Garrett and Dakota a few steps behind her, Layla went toward the one on the right.

"Now let's just hope they've still got that job waiting for me," she said, pushing open the saloon door.

Four

The Scarlet Dream

They paused at the doorway, glancing about in surprise. It was anything but the kind of establishment one might expect to find in a little town like New Eden. The room was immense and grandly furnished. In front, its long wooden surface smooth, highly polished, stood the bar. The remainder of floor space was devoted to tables, more than fifty of them, each the same size, capable of seating four. Toward the rear, larger tables, serving a different purpose, were provided—for roulette, dice, cards. At the front of a winding stairway that led to a narrow balcony, a wheel of fortune towered above the gaming tables, its face white, the numbers a striking crimson.

High-ceilinged, decorated everywhere with bright, rich reds, the Scarlet Palace Saloon offered its customers a place of refuge from the dreariness of everyday life. In this great pleasure hall, diversions of all sorts could be pursued amidst surroundings of flashy splendor. Though empty for the most part now—only a few solitary drinkers were at the tables; the gamblers had not yet arrived to try their luck; the piano in back was silent—it was not difficult to imagine what it would be like here on busy nights. The stillness that lingered in the air seemed merely temporary, sooner or later to be broken by a swelling clamor of activity.

Impressed by what they saw, the three travelers exchanged a wordless, yet all-expressive look. They released the doors, which quickly snapped closed behind them, and went in.

The bartender, a large-framed, balding man, was at the

far end of the bar, arranging bottles on the shelves. When he noticed the strangers in the mirror that ran along the wall, he turned, greeted them with a slight toss of his head, and said in a perfunctory tone, "What can I do for you?"

"Is Marcus Tanner around?" asked Layla.

The bartender studied her a moment before replying, "Hold on." He leaned over the bar and called, "Hey, Marc!"

In an isolated corner across the room, two men were working at a paper-cluttered table, a set of ledgers spread out before them. Preoccupied, one of them answered without looking around, "Yeah?"

"Someone here to see you," said the bartender.

The two men glanced up from the books and turned their gazes on the newcomers.

"Okay. Just a minute," Tanner told them. He made a few notations on a scrap of paper, concluded what he and the second man had been discussing, then pushed back his chair and got up.

He was tall and lean-featured, in his late thirties. His clothing, meticulously tailored for a perfect fit, was flashy, expensive-looking. The closely trimmed moustache he wore—like his hair, a dark black—gave him a ruggedly handsome appearance. And he seemed well aware of this. With a self-confident manner that bordered on haughtiness, he came up to the bar and said, "I'm Tanner. How can I help you?"

When Layla told him her name he said, "Oh, yes, I got your wire the other day. I was expecting you."

For a fraction of an instant, his eyes wandered down the length of her body. Just as momentary was the trace of a grin that formed on his lips. Layla caught the look and understood what it meant. He was satisfied with what he saw. She had passed inspection.

Neither resenting him nor overly pleased that he had granted his approval, Layla said casually, as though she hadn't noticed, "And these are a couple of friends of mine."

Tanner gave Garrett and Dakota a short nod. "Pleased to know you." Returning to Layla, he asked, "You just get in on the stage? It's a little later than usual."

"It's going to be a lot later than usual," Layla answered. "About a *week* later, as a matter of fact." In response to Tanner's uncomprehending expression, she briefly related what had happened.

At the conclusion of the narrative, Tanner remarked, "Well, it sounds like you had a pretty rough time of it today."

"It was rough enough, all right," Layla said, seeing her chance to bring up the most pressing topic on her mind, the reason she had come to New Eden in the first place. "I just hope things will be a little better around here."

Tanner smiled. "I'm sure you'll find it more to your liking. We don't have trouble here very often. And when we do, it's nothing like that. But don't take my word for it. Wait until you talk with the other girls who work here. They'll tell you the same thing."

His answer put Layla at ease. There was no need to inquire. The job was already hers.

"How many of them are there?" she asked in a pleasant voice.

"Seven. But we can always use one more."

"I'm glad to hear that. I wouldn't have wanted to come all this way for nothing."

Standing beside them, idly listening to their conversation, Garrett felt uncomfortable, out of place. He began to regret his decision to accompany Layla into the saloon. After all, he told himself, he had guessed the line of work she was in. He and Dakota should have left her at the door and gone their separate way.

He waited for a suitable opportunity to break into the discussion, and when it first presented itself said, "Well, I think we'll leave the two of you alone so you can talk over business."

Surprised, Layla said, "Why? Where are you going?"

Garrett understood from the spontaneity of her reaction, the hint of concern in her tone, that she did not want him to leave. And in that same instant he realized something else: neither did he. The urge to remain with her was sudden, and he found himself succumbing to it.

"Sure, stick around," Tanner said amiably. "Let me buy you a drink. It's the least I can do after you helped the young lady get here safe and sound." Turning, he moved up to the bar.

"Set up a round of drinks for all of us, Bill."

Garrett made no objection. He would let events run their course. Attempting, unsuccessfully, to provide a reason for this choice, his train of thought veered off in another direction, leading him to something Marta had said that morning: *Decisions are often made without our knowledge of the why or how. We do certain things without questioning ourselves. Something tells us that we should, and we do it.*

Regardless of how he felt about Marta's more superstitious remarks, on this subject Garrett could not have agreed with her more. A passive wait-and-see attitude was definitely in order.

The bartender came over with a bottle and four glasses and started pouring the drinks. Hesitating before filling the last glass, he looked across at Dakota and said, "Do you want this too?"

"That'll be fine," the sandy-haired youth replied with reserve.

Questioningly, the bartender's gaze shifted to Garrett.

"It's all right," said Garrett. "He's had it before."

"I'd be surprised if he hadn't, at his age," Tanner chuckled. "Go ahead, Bill. He's old enough to have what he wants."

"Okay, okay," the bartender said quickly, defensively. "I was just asking."

"It doesn't matter," Dakota responded, offering a smile. "No harm done."

With an approving nod, Tanner said to Garrett, "Yeah, he's old enough."

When the bartender was finished, Tanner picked up his glass and motioned them away from the bar. "Come on, let's go over there and take a load off our feet."

The others took their drinks and followed him across the room. Tanner went toward the table at which he had been working before. The second man was still there, his face buried in the ledgers.

Coming up from behind, Tanner gave him a hearty slap on the back. "Well, Jase, how's it going?"

The man turned quickly, startled. "Oh, all right. I've almost got them balanced. I should be finished soon."

Tanner leaned over his associate's shoulder and, briefly inspecting the columns of figures, murmured, "Good, good." Then, straightening himself, he suggested, "Here, why don't you leave the rest of this till later and join us for a while. There's someone here I think you might want to meet."

The second man glanced around, past Tanner, not having noticed the three who stood there until now.

"Why, yes, certainly," he said. He removed his reading glasses and briskly rose from the chair. He was of about the same age as Tanner, somewhat shorter, evidently quite a bit less outgoing. He was dressed conservatively, in a somber brown business suit. As expertly made, perhaps, as Tanner's, but on his slender frame the clothing was wasted.

Tanner took a step or two back and said as he came up beside the others, "This is my partner, Jason Pratt. Jase, this is Layla Magnum, who's going to be working for us. And these are—you know, I never did catch your names," he told Garrett, who then completed the introductions.

With a polite smile, Pratt said, "I'm glad to meet all of you," and began exchanging handshakes with them. As he did so, he peered at each of them intently, unafraid of meeting their gazes. His eyes alert, intelligent, he seemed to be fixing their faces in his mind.

When he came to Dakota, he asked, mildly curious, "Are you Mr. Garrett's son?"

"Everyone asks us that," Dakota replied, darting Layla a look. "No, we're not related. We're partners—like the two of you."

"I see, I see," Pratt said, though he didn't really.

Tanner ushered them over to an empty table and pulled up a fifth chair for himself. After they had settled into place, Pratt turned to Layla, who was seated beside him, and said in a cordial tone, "Tell me, Miss Magnum, where are you from?"

"No one place in particular. I've been traveling around since I was about eighteen. Before coming here I was working up in Cheyenne."

"That's supposed to be nice country around there. I

can't say I've ever been up that way myself, but I've heard a lot about it."

"I liked living there," Layla said. "Prettier than most areas I've been to. Even so, after a while I decided it was time to move on."

"And what brought you to these parts?"

"Why, the job *here* did," she answered in surprise.

Pratt, too, was puzzled. "What do you mean? I'm not sure I follow—"

"Don't you remember? I mentioned her to you," Tanner interrupted. "She wrote us about a month ago. She'd met Sam Reaves, who told her we were looking for people to work here."

"Oh, yes," Pratt said, suddenly recalling. "I thought her name sounded familiar." Then, to Layla: "How's Sam doing, anyway? We haven't heard from him in a while now."

"He looked like he was in good shape," Layla smiled. "I didn't really get much of a chance to know him, though. He was just passing through."

"That sounds just like what he wanted to do. He left New Eden toward the end of summer with nothing else in mind but to roam around and see what there is to see. I'll tell you, I wouldn't mind trying something like that myself one day."

Pratt then returned to the subject of Layla's own travels. He had moved to New Eden five years ago, he explained, and in all that time he had not ventured more than twenty miles from the town in any direction. Responsibilities of one sort or another had always prevented him from doing so. Because of this, he went on, he wanted to learn as much as he could about the various places he'd never had the chance to visit. Hearing about them was a poor substitute for the real thing, he admitted, but all the same it was still better than remaining in ignorance of what was going on around him.

Layla, then Garrett and Dakota as well, responded indulgently to each of Pratt's questions. Though he struck them as somewhat absentminded, they found his ingenuous manner refreshing. And, more than that, they shared with Pratt a common ground: they were all drifters at heart. Sitting back, taking the opportunity to relax from the

60

day's ride, they obliged the man who lived in a world of dreams by relating to him some of their experiences.

For Tanner, though, it was just so much small talk, for which he had little taste. After putting up with it for fifteen minutes, he interrupted Pratt once again, this time with obvious impatience.

"They've been riding all day, Jase," he said, his voice restrained, patronizing. "Why don't we save some of this for another time?"

"Ah, he's just not as interested as I am," Pratt said laughingly to the others.

Soured by the whole matter, Tanner did not make any response. Instead, he asked Layla, "Do you want to start tonight?"

"Well, sure," she answered, taken aback by his abruptness. "I can't see why not."

"Okay, then I imagine you'll want to rest up a bit first," Tanner decided for her.

He tilted back his chair and called across the bar, "Scanlon!" He made a beckoning motion with his arm.

The bartender put down what he was doing and came over to their table.

"Go up and see if you can find Ginger," Tanner said to him. "Tell her I want to see her. I'll keep an eye on things while you're gone."

"And if she isn't there?"

"Then get Sally or Laura May."

Scanlon nodded, walked to the far corner of the room, and ascended the winding flight of stairs. Reaching the landing, he went in through a door that stood at the end of the narrow balcony.

"Where does that lead?" Garrett asked.

"Into the hotel," said Tanner.

"It's what you might call a kind of shortcut," Pratt added. "It takes you up to the rooms on the second floor."

"You own this and the hotel?"

"That's right." As he was answering, Tanner turned from Garrett and looked toward the entrance in front. Someone had just come in and was going up to the bar.

"I'll be right back," Tanner muttered ill-temperedly. He got up from the table and went to see after the customer.

Garrett watched him for a moment and then glanced

about the saloon. "Tell me," he said, "how long have you had this place?"

"Well, let's see," Pratt replied. "Come the spring, it'll be four years. We had it built ourselves, you know. According to our own specifications."

"You had it all planned out beforehand, huh?" Garrett chuckled.

"Whatever work you put into it, I'd say it was worth the trouble," Layla noted. "I've not seen too many places fixed up as nice as this."

"We're proud of it," said Pratt. "It's something we'd always wanted to do. We were just waiting until we had enough money. You see, Marc and I are more than business partners. We've known each other since we were kids. We grew up together."

"Around here?"

"No, no, Miss Magnum. We're from back East originally."

A short while after Tanner returned to the table, the bartender appeared at the head of the stairs. With him was a tall, blond woman. Though she was almost forty, the years had done little to diminish her womanly appeal. Her figure was full and shapely, with more than a suggestion of sensuality in its soft fleshiness. Able to maintain a friendly, agreeable disposition while at the same time communicating a powerful sense of self-mastery, she was in confident possession of the secret of her sex.

Briefly running through the round of introductions a second time, Tanner then told her, "I'd like you to take Layla upstairs and help her get settled."

"All right," Ginger replied. "Be glad to."

"Go on up with her," Tanner said to Layla. "She'll answer any questions you might have."

"You don't have to worry about that," Ginger said with a wink. "I'll fill her in on everything she's got to know."

Pratt stood up with Layla and pulled back her chair. "Then I guess we'll be seeing you in a little while. I hope you'll enjoy working here."

"Thanks. So do I." Layla then asked Garrett, who had also risen, "What about you? Will you be here later on?"

"I think so. It's getting sort of late to start going anywhere now," he said. "How do you feel about it, Dakota?"

For a reason similar to Garrett's, although approached from a different age and with different desires, Dakota, too, wished to remain in town. He wanted to see more of Layla, to learn more about the kind of life she led. He had never known anyone like her, and in him was the distinct awareness that he had been missing something.

"Sure, let's stay," he replied. "I don't mind."

"Well, there you are," said Garrett.

Layla smiled. "Good."

She picked up her bag and followed Ginger to the stairs. When they came up onto the balcony, Layla paused a moment. She leaned against the wooden railing and peered out across the spacious room. Her gaze wandered thoughtfully about. Gradually it came to rest on Garrett.

Ginger walked on to the door and pulled it open. "This way," she called cheerily.

Layla turned and went in.

Garrett watched until the door closed after her. "Well, if we're going to be staying," he then said, "I guess we ought to see about getting ourselves some rooms. You're not all booked up, are you?"

"No, no, far from it," Pratt answered with amusement. "You'll have more than enough to choose from. Business in the hotel's been a little slow lately. Right now, it's pretty much just the girls we've got staying there."

"In the hotel?"

"Yes, upstairs," Pratt responded, seeing nothing strange in the idea.

"I reckon we're going to have some nice neighbors, don't you think?" Garrett said to Dakota.

The youth smiled.

With another glance around, Garrett remarked, "Judging from the look of things, I'd say business wasn't too good in here either."

"That's because it's the afternoon," said Pratt. "We never get many people in around this time. But come back in a couple of hours, Mr. Garrett. After nightfall. You'll see. Everything will be a lot different then."

Five

The Slash of a Knife

Dakota sat back, his plate scraped clean. With curiosity, he looked to the other side of the table and watched as Garrett continued eating. He followed every movement closely, more attentively than Garrett's handling of the knife and fork warranted. Something else was on the youth's mind.

"Garrett?" he asked, edging forward in his seat. "What do you think of her?"

Garrett glanced up. "Think of who?"

"You know who I mean. Layla."

"I like her," Garrett replied, and returned to his food. "Why? Don't you?"

"I'm not really sure. She's nice, I'll say that. And interesting to listen to. But . . ."

"But what?"

"Well, you know . . . the kind of work she does and all. Actually, she's nothing more than a dance-hall girl."

"Nothing more than that?" Garrett said with an indulgent smile. "You didn't feel that way about her before we reached town, did you?"

"How could I have? I didn't know until we all got to the saloon this afternoon."

"Then don't let it make that much of a difference to you now."

"Doesn't her job bother you?"

"I don't see why it should. It doesn't seem to bother *her* any."

Gathering the last morsels of meat and gravy-soaked vegetables onto his fork, Garrett continued, "Try looking at it the other way around. What if everything else that happened today was the same except that when we rode into town it turned out that Layla was—oh, a schoolteacher, let's say. Would *that* have all of a sudden made her into a different person than the one you met this morning? Or made you like her any more or less than you already did?"

"No, I guess not," Dakota laughed. "I can't imagine her as a schoolteacher, though."

"All right, then you might as well accept her for what she is. A dance-hall girl. You can't change things anyway, so don't bother trying."

Dakota's eyes wandered down to the table. Absently, he toyed with the knife on his plate. "Okay," he said, smiling when he looked up, "I guess you're right."

Garrett sensed that Dakota had understood, and let the matter go at that. Finishing his meal, he pushed aside the earthenware dinner plate and drank down his coffee.

"You have enough to eat?"

"Sure, it was plenty," Dakota answered, in spirits somewhat higher than before. For the present at least, he found Garrett's answers to be satisfactory, and allowed them to free him from the burden of his thoughts.

"I should imagine it was," said Garrett. "What with that extra helping of yours, you had enough for three."

Dakota shrugged his shoulders. "I was hungry."

"I gathered."

They called over the woman who had served them and paid the bill. When they emerged from the restaurant, Garrett stretched and took a deep breath of the night air.

"Where would you like to go now?" he asked.

Dakota gazed in the direction of the Scarlet Palace Saloon. Rays of golden light were streaming through its windows and doors, throwing a soft, amorphous glow on the ground outside. He made out the sounds of a piano, of raised voices. Equally roisterous, they seemed to be calling to him, luring him on.

"It looks to me like that's the only place in town where anything's going on," he remarked suggestively.

Garrett grinned. "You want to see what it's like, don't you?"

"Well, we told Layla we'd be back around now," said the youth. "And anyway, it could be interesting."

They turned from the restaurant and started down the block. The walks creaked hollowly at their step; the steady rhythm of footfalls carried into the night. One after another in a long row, the stores they passed were closed, and the little that could be seen of their dark interiors was cold and cavernous. Among the buildings lights could be seen burning here and there in upper-story windows; shadows flitting across drawn shades gave an additional indication of activity within. Outside, however, there was neither life nor warmth. But for the presence of one person who had been careful to avoid the notice of Garrett and Dakota, the streets were empty.

With each approaching step they took, the assortment of barroom noises became louder, more discordant. The exuberant message rang in Dakota's ears and filled him with excitement. His pace quickened.

"Listen, if you want to have something to drink, go ahead," Garrett advised him as they were nearing the saloon. "But make sure to keep an eye on yourself."

Dakota smiled. "You don't have to worry about that."

"Good enough. I just want you to keep it in mind, so you won't go ordering more than you can handle. I don't want you getting yourself sick from it or anything."

"How much do you think I'm going to have?" Dakota said, amused at the nature of Garrett's concern. "Do you want to know something? To be honest, I don't even really like the way the stuff tastes. There's no way I could drink enough of it to get sick. I wouldn't want to."

"That's good to hear. It's not at all a bad thing to dislike. Go on like that, and you'll save yourself a lot of money in the end."

"Well, I'm glad to see I set your mind at rest on that count."

"That you did. But one thing—" Garrett added, his features arched with suspicion, "—if memory serves me right, didn't you have yourself a healthy couple of drinks just this afternoon?"

"Oh, that was something else altogether. I only wanted to see if it was as bad as I remembered," Dakota said, and

66

the wry smiles he and Garrett had been wearing were swept away in a gust of laughter.

And across the street, clinging to the shadows, following Garrett and Dakota, someone made a hurried dart into the darkened doorway of a store just opposite the town's grand casino-bar. Pressing close against the wall, he watched, waited.

With all its costly fixtures and flashy embellishments, the Scarlet Palace Saloon had nonetheless not fully presented its true character that afternoon. For in daylight, despite its furnishings, it had been a room, larger than many, more fancily decorated than many, but still merely a room. And a fairly cold one at that. But now, playing host to voices and music that battled each other for clamorous supremacy, circulating drink-filled glasses with easy efficiency to all at the party, it had become something more than an inanimate enclosure. Surrounded by eager spectators, its gaming tables had become stages on which kings, queens and deuces acted out their roles to the excitement of all. The bar, which had seemed longer when fewer people were standing at it, had become a wellspring of tipsy forgetfulness against which many thirstily pressed. And in back, hovering, watching over all, the once-idle wheel of fortune spun in a wild dancing blur of colors and numbers.

It was not until the descent of darkness, when the presence of sumptuous lamplight could transform surroundings by drenching them with rich, unnatural hues, that the Scarlet Palace came forth and displayed its splendor, revealing itself as possessor of an irresistibly ebullient life all its own.

As he followed Garrett in from the street and the double doors swung around and past him, Dakota felt as he had when, at an earlier and more tender age, he had summoned up the courage to make his first entrance into a saloon. Many years had passed since then, and he had seen scores of saloons in scores of different towns. And, moreover, he had been into this particular one only a few hours ago. But the facts of his past became suddenly irrelevant. This was a new experience—bright, fresh, exciting.

No sooner had he taken a step inside than the lusty array of barroom sounds seemed to reach a sudden crescendo. Having enticed him from down the street with their raw liveliness, they now surged and crested all at once and came crashing down upon him with the force of an angry ocean wave.

"Hey, Laura May," a sodden voice bellowed, "come on over and give us a little of your sweet company!"

"He was bluffin', just plain bluffin'! I knew it all along!" came the victorious cry from among a circle of card players.

"Yeah, I know your kind," a woman's voice, no less loud and hearty than the rest, taunted laughingly from the wheel of fortune. "Try putting your money where your mouth is! Who knows, maybe I'll bring you a little luck!"

An unrelated burst of laughter sprang up from a different corner, only to be drowned in turn by another series of high-spirited calls:

"Place yer bets! Ya don't play, ya don't win!"

"Ah, I don't believe a word of it! You were just making it up as you went along!"

"Bet you she does! They all do! All you need's the money!"

"Make it another round for all of us! No, forget it—bring us the bottle instead!"

And, over and over again in ceaseless repetition, the piano in back kept everything bouncing to the tune of "Camptown Races."

For the regulars at the bar and tables, this was all a mere backdrop, something hardly worthy of notice. It was a basic and necessary part of the festive atmosphere they sought out consistently night after night, but, being no more than this, was far from the center of attention. It was as much taken for granted as the red-bathed furnishings that surrounded them everywhere.

But Dakota saw it differently. Being a newcomer and an outsider, he had little else to focus upon. He became keenly aware of everything that was going on about him. The laughter, the voices, the music—all gradually seemed to merge into one, forming a broad wall of sound. And he was on the other side of this wall, separated from the actual participants in these noisy rites.

Dakota followed close behind Garrett, weaving his way through what appeared to be an endless maze of men, tables and chairs. Bent on reaching his goal without jostling anyone, he watched where he put his feet and kept his elbows stiffly at his sides. He wanted to remain a spectator, and to accomplish this he thought it best to try to be as invisible as possible.

When he and Garrett reached an empty space at the far end of the bar, the youth squeezed into place, standing sideways with his back to an old man who was drinking alone and was passing the time by grumbling oaths under his breath. Carefully steering clear of him, Dakota attempted to make himself comfortable. He languidly dropped an arm across the edge of the glass-laden bar top. Next, he discovered a brass railing below, and rested a foot upon it. He ended by shifting his weight onto these two limbs and leaning his side into the bar. Satisfied with the relaxed attitude he had struck up, he turned to Garrett, who, less self-consciously, had settled himself into the space available to him.

"So how do you like it?" asked Garrett.

"Fine," Dakota smiled. "A little crowded though."

While Garrett was busy trying to get the bartender's attention, Dakota scanned the room once again. Conscious that his new vantage point placed him right in the center of things, he felt a redoubling of his excitement and interest.

The men who filled the saloon were of all ages and occupations, from ranch hands to shopkeepers, from drifters to bank presidents. Dakota had the impression he could guess their life histories just by looking at them. He may not have been as well educated as others his age, nor had as many friends, but in the last few of his sixteen years of life he had roamed widely with Garrett, and had seen the counterparts of these men many times before. As he watched them indulge in their sports, Dakota was struck by the roughness of male mannerisms, the brutal simplicity of the amusements they pursued. He tried to imagine himself at their age, doing what they were doing, but met with little success. This realization left him with a vague sense of apprehension.

If his thoughts came quickly while looking at the men, they sped hypnotically through his mind when his eyes fastened on the women who worked there. Their scant, scarlet-colored dance-hall costumes enthralled him—less so, however, than what they left exposed. Most of the women were of about Layla's age, but there was one in her early twenties, blonde and slender, who appeared to be quite popular. Her name was Laura May, Dakota gathered from the men's repeated calls for her attention. More appealing in the youth's eyes, though, was Ginger, whom Dakota recalled from that afternoon, and who, like the Scarlet Palace itself, seemed to take on additional life and color with the coming of nightfall. Perhaps twenty years older than Laura May, Ginger nonetheless held Dakota's attention for many minutes together with the manner in which she carried herself, a manner saturated with an extravagant vibrancy all her own.

And then he caught sight of Layla. Sitting for the past few minutes with a well-dressed gambler at the roulette wheel, she had just gotten up and was now winding her way among the tables, stopping here and there to chat with the men.

Just as one can feel something without actually understanding the content of those feelings, Dakota suddenly felt, while barely grasping, the reason why tonight's was so different from all other experiences he'd had in saloons. And Layla was for him the embodiment of that reason. His period as onlooker to the rituals of masculinity was drawing to a close. The rawness of youth would soon become a painful burden, and it would then be time for him to take his place, in his own way, in the world of men.

Dakota did not notice when the bartender came over with the drinks. He was entranced at the sight of the woman, and as he looked at her, barely clothed by comparison with the way he had seen her earlier, his thoughts kept returning to the fight she'd had with Cantrill that morning. The image of her and the one-armed man tossing and squirming in the dust would not leave his mind.

"Here we are," Garrett said, and handed him his drink. He noticed the direction of Dakota's gaze and added, "Whatever you said about her before, you still have to admit she's real pretty to look at."

Dakota smiled and nodded.

While Garrett and Dakota stood at the bar, watching the goings-on about them, they were in turn being watched from outside. His figure draped in shadow, someone was huddled by the corner of the saloon window, silently peering in.

As he crouched there with one cheek pressed up against the pane, regarding everything through a squinted left eye, he looked as though he were peeking through the keyhole of a door. Except for an occasional glance about to see if anyone was coming up behind him, he remained motionless. His watchful stare was filled with a single-minded determination, but otherwise there was no sign of emotion on his features.

He had taken up this position nearly fifteen minutes ago, shortly after Garrett and Dakota had gone inside. His surveillance of the two continued an additional few minutes until a group of horsemen could be heard coming down the deserted streets. The youth whirled at the sound of the approaching hoofbeats and, hobbling quickly away, disappeared into the darkness.

"What do you say we go over there and sit down?" Garrett said, motioning with his glass. Across the room, three men were getting up to go try their luck at the wheel of fortune. Drinks in hand, he and Dakota made their way over and took the table.

From their new places they noticed Marcus Tanner standing on the balcony that overlooked the saloon. Dressed for the occasion in suitably flashy attire, he was leaning against the railing, watching everything with the calm benevolence of one who knows that he is to get half the night's profits. When Tanner saw them, he nodded, then continued surveying his spacious domain.

"There's someone who knows what business to be in," observed Garrett.

"Yeah, I guess so," Dakota replied abstractedly, his gaze already moving elsewhere. He was still searching the room, trying to catch a fresh glimpse of Layla, when he felt that someone was coming up behind him.

"Well, how are you enjoying yourselves?"

Dakota was caught by surprise. A quick flutter running

through him, he managed to meet Layla's eyes and utter a few words of greeting.

"Would you like to join us for a while?" Garrett suggested.

"I can't see why not, seeing as how you're paying guests in this establishment," Layla replied with a grin, and drew up a chair.

Dakota watched her with fascination. Everything about her was so infallibly natural, and this made his reactions to her all the more baffling.

"How are things going?" Garrett was saying. "Do you think you're going to like it?"

"Oh, it'll probably work out all right. Judging from the looks of things, I'll be kept pretty busy most of the time."

"It sure does have its share of customers, doesn't it?"

"Well, that's what it's all about," said Layla. "If things were any different, I'd start thinking about finding a job somewhere else."

"Then you think you're going to stay?" Dakota asked.

"For a while at least."

Their conversation was interrupted by one of a group of ranch hands at a nearby table. "Hey, Layla, where you keepin' yourself? Come on over!"

"Yeah, c'mon!" echoed another. "We'll buy you a drink!"

"Looks like you've already made yourself a couple of friends," Garrett remarked drily.

"Like I said before," Layla said as she pushed back her chair and rose, "that's what it's all about."

Then, before moving away, her expression changed. "I'll be back later. All right?"

Garrett smiled. "Sure, see you then."

Dakota studied both of them with curiosity. He waited until Layla had joined the others before asking, "Garrett? Doesn't that bother you?"

Garrett looked at him. "No, it doesn't, boy. That's her job," he said in a measured tone. "And besides, I don't have any claim on her."

"And what if you did?" Dakota asked, a look of perplexity knitting his youthful features. "How would you feel then?"

"Listen, let me tell you something. There are certain

kinds of women who won't let you put your brand on them and herd them around like cattle. And Layla's one of them. Either you take her as she is or you forget her. But you never try to change her. It won't work."

Frank Wilson, the Scarlet Palace Hotel's middle-aged desk clerk, was busy tidying up the lobby when the front door opened and a strange-looking youth hurriedly limped inside. A startled gasp escaped from the bespectacled clerk's lips when he caught sight of the stranger.

"You run this place?"

"I work here," Wilson timidly replied. "What can I do for you?"

The youth slammed the door, grabbed Wilson by the lapels of his jacket, and dragged him away from the windows.

"What—what's the matter?" stammered Wilson. "What did I do?"

"I want you t' answer a couple of questions for me," the other hissed in a sharp undertone, tightening his grip on the clerk. His face, gaunt and misshapen, was pressed close upon Wilson's.

"Sure, sure, what do you want to know?"

"Some people came into town today. One of them's a man dressed in black, the other's a kid. You know 'em?"

"Yes, I know them, I know them. Why?"

"Why?" The twisted gaze narrowed. " 'Cause they're a real cute couple and I wanna get to know 'em better, that's why. Hey, listen—" With this he began shaking the terrified clerk. The next thing Wilson knew, there was a knife pressing at his neck. "I ain't got all day. Where are they stayin'?"

"Up-upstairs. Second floor. Rooms fourteen and fifteen."

"Fourteen and fifteen, huh? That's better. And what about the woman with them?"

"Woman? What woman? They came in alone!"

The knife began to dig at his flesh. "Listen, I ain't gonna ask again. A woman came in today. She's nice and pretty, just the kind you'd wanna be with when you get

73

tired of yer wife. She's right next door, working in the saloon. Now where—"

"Oh, you mean Miss Magnum. She's got room nineteen. Same floor. But I wasn't lying. She didn't come in with those other two."

"Forget it. Now one last thing. Where can I find a doctor around here?"

"A-A doctor?"

"Yeah, that's right." He gave Wilson's head a downward shove, and pointed with the knife at the blood-stained bandages wrapped around his leg. "They put a bullet in me and I want to get it out. Now where do I go?"

"Doc Winslow's. Outside and to your left. Just keep going. You can't miss it. It's the big white house with a fence around it."

"Good, good." The birdlike, miscast eye darted him a menacing look. "Now you ain't gonna tell them people I'm looking for 'em, are you? Not after I've gone and told you how it was them who shot me. Huh?"

"No, no. You can be certain of that. I give you my word."

"Fine, I'm glad you said that. Puts my mind at ease. But just t' make sure—" Once again the hand snatched Wilson by the jacket.

"Hey, what—what are you doing?" Wilson cried as he was pulled across the room. "I said—"

"I know what you said. Just git down there behind the desk. Flat on your stomach."

"But why?"

"Go ahead. Just do what I tell you and you won't have nothin' to worry about. It ain't you I want."

"Okay, okay. But please . . . don't hurt me." Trembling under the prodding of the knife, the hotel clerk dropped down to his knees.

"Like this?" he called behind him from his prostrate position.

"Yeah, that's fine, just fine," Willy Lavery drawled in an amiable tone, then plunged the blade into the man's back. Frank Wilson groaned. His body shuddered convulsively. At the third thrust he fell still.

"That'll keep you. They won't find you here for a while," the youth muttered as he crammed the body further under the desk with the flat of his boot. His eye darting cautiously around for signs of witnesses, he hurried out into the night.

Unlike his partner, Jason Pratt made it a nightly practice to wander about the saloon and mix with his customers. When he reached Garrett and Dakota's table, he dropped his hand on the man's shoulder as if they were old friends and said, "Well, was I wrong? It's a little different at night, isn't it?"

"You'll find no arguments on that score," Garrett admitted with a smile.

"What about you, boy? Ever seen a place like this before?"

"No, I can't say I have," Dakota replied, and shared a grin with Garrett.

When they invited him to join them, Pratt pulled up a chair and immediately launched into his favorite topic of conversation.

"So tell me about some of the places you've been to, Mr. Garrett."

While they were talking, a thin, sober-faced woman appeared at the saloon doors. The regulars at the bar knew who she was, and consequently attached little significance to her entrance into the men-filled room. One of the older, more gentlemanly among them called to her as she passed:

"Good evening, Mrs. Pratt. How are you tonight?"

The woman granted him the faintest hint of a smile and continued on her way. Her gaze fixed on her husband, she moved through the crowd of men briskly, indifferent to their presence. There was a grim austerity in her bearing that made her seem older, less appealing than her years might have allowed her. Like her husband of five years, she had grown up back East. But for her the change of environment had not proven beneficial. The new life had robbed her of her looks, leaving her frail and sallow.

Pratt stopped in mid-sentence when he saw her approaching. For a brief, uncomfortable instant, conflicting feelings of love and apprehension rose to the surface. The corners of his lips drew back stiffly, hovering indecisively between a smile and frown.

Mrs. Pratt came abruptly to a halt a few feet from him and said, "Jason, I'd like to speak with you a few minutes—outside."

"Why? Is something the matter?"

"Please!" she answered, with obvious restraint. She turned for the door and began retracing her steps through the crowd.

Stunned, Pratt sat there for a moment, the blood rushing to his cheeks. "I'm—I'm sorry. Please excuse me," he muttered absently to the two seated beside him. He rose hurriedly and followed after his wife.

"Whew, he's sure in for it," said Dakota.

"That's the way it looks, all right," Garrett agreed.

Dakota watched as the couple, separated by about ten paces, but each moving the same course, made their way outside.

"Garrett," he asked after a brief hesitation, "is that always what it's like when people get married?"

The man turned to him and smiled. "Depends on the people, wouldn't you think?"

When Pratt came outside, he found his wife already in tears.

"Janet? What is it?" He reached out tentatively to her, but, shrinking back, retracted his hand and reached for his handkerchief instead.

"Please stop crying," he said quietly. "Here, take this."

"It seems as if all I'm doing is crying lately," she replied, while trying to compose herself. She took the handkerchief, wiped her eyes, and drew a deep breath.

She then continued, more calmly. "I'm sorry. I didn't mean to make a scene. But I couldn't help it. I couldn't wait until you got home. Do you understand me, Jason? I just couldn't bear it any longer. Not alone. I had to see you."

"Why? What is it?" her husband repeated anxiously. This time he reached out and touched her arm. "Tell me, Janet."

She searched his face tenderly. Tears once again began to well up in her eyes, but she wiped them away. She lowered her gaze and spoke slowly, in a voice that strained for control over her feelings.

"It isn't going to work, Jason. I'm not happy with the way things are. I don't mean to put the blame on you, because in a way it's more my fault. I should have done more for myself, but I didn't. Instead I tried to accommodate myself to your way of doing things, and now I know that that was a mistake."

Her words burned through Jason. "I—I don't understand. Haven't I always shown you how much you mean to me? Do you doubt my love for you?"

Janet Pratt smiled sadly. "No, it isn't that. I know that you love me. But sometimes love is just not enough. A person needs fulfillment just as much. Fulfillment, Jason, that's what I don't have and what I need most. Do you know, in all these years, I don't think I've done one thing I wanted to, one thing just for myself. We came out here as soon as we were married and—and I think that's the trouble. It wasn't a good idea right from the start."

"But you wanted to come here as much as I did," he protested.

The sad smile returned to her face. "I know, and that's why I'm not blaming you. We both wanted to try to make the dream work."

"And didn't it?" Pratt glanced proudly at the large building behind them.

"But it was *your* dream, Jason. Yours and Marc's. It was something the two of you always wanted. I had no part in it. I just came along for the ride as your wife. And look at how things are now—," here the chill of a bitter anger filled her eyes and voice, "—this business takes up all of your time, and I'm left with nothing to do at all. Why—why, you're so busy, I had to come over and take you away from those wretched people in there if I wanted to talk with you!"

"Wretched people? Well, that's some way—"

"Oh, what's the difference? Let's say they're all very fine people. The point is, you have them to talk with, and you certainly seem to enjoy it, judging from the amount of time you spend there. But I have no one, except you, no friends at all. I don't belong here, Jason. These aren't my kind of people, and this isn't the kind of life for me."

"And what makes you think I'm so pleased with the way things are?" Jason broke in. "Let me tell you something. I've been tied down to this place ever since we started building it. It's never given me any time to myself. And it was for you that I did it. Because that's the way I thought things should be done. Should be done! Hell, I never gave any time to the way I *wanted* them done.

"Marc, he's satisfied. Day after day, night after night, the same thing over and over again. And the money always pouring in. But I want something a little more than money. I want to get out and see something outside of this little flea-bitten town. There's a lot of country out there, and I don't think I've seen one-tenth of what I ought to have by now."

The woman closed her eyes and tried to make sense of it all. Sacrifices. Their lives together seemed like nothing more than one long series of sacrifices.

"Well, I guess we're each prisoners in our own way," she said with a grim sigh.

"Maybe so," Jason Pratt nodded. "May—"

He froze, transfixed by the sight of the glow coming from the far end of town.

"My God," his wife whispered when she turned.

In that instant, as they watched the flames licking the windows of the large white house and rising into the sky, they forgot their own troubles. Pratt whirled and ran into the saloon.

"Everybody! Quick! Doc Winslow's place is on fire!"

The men poured out of the saloon, but by the time they reached the house it was already too late. The fire roared and danced, and the fated home soon disappeared behind the flames. An anxious volley of shouts rose from the steadily growing crowd.

"What happened to the Doc? Was he inside?"

"Hey, someone oughta go tell the sheriff! He ain't here yet!"

"Come on, let's get some buckets and make sure it doesn't spread!"

In a matter of minutes, the fiery skeleton of the house trembled and collapsed upon itself. The hastily formed bucket brigade could do little but drench the embers and contain the flames.

Later, when the neighboring houses were safe from danger and all that remained of the doctor's home was smoldering rubble, the people of New Eden gathered in the center of the main street. They milled about restlessly, a ceaseless repetition of questions rising from their midst. For each of them, the peaceful security upon which they based their day-to-day lives had been rudely disturbed. Frightened, in need of reassurance, they did as many would do in their places. They turned to the law.

It took Jack Graham, the sheriff of New Eden, more than a few minutes to get the crowd settled. Tall, lean-featured, he had the hard look of a man who had spent his earlier years taming wild stallions, and now, perhaps seeking a better source of income, had taken on the more difficult job of taming men.

"C'mon, keep it down!" he kept shouting in a bad-tempered growl, not really knowing what the people wanted from him in the first place. As far as he was concerned, the fire had been an accident, and there was little the law could do about accidents.

"There, that's better," he said when at last the clamor began to subside. "Keep it that way. Now . . . who saw the doc last?"

"I keep telling you!" a woman called out. "He was home all night. I could see the lights burning in his windows."

"All right, all right," Graham said, trying to keep everyone calm, "then I reckon all we can do is suppose he was in there when the place went up."

"Then he's dead?" a nervous voice exclaimed.

"I don't see what else there is to think," the sheriff replied with a toss of his shoulders.

"Do you reckon it was an accident, sheriff?"

"Well, there weren't any shots fired, were there? And nobody saw anyone going in or out of the place."

"I think you may be wrong, Graham. There's a good chance it wasn't an accident."

A haggard expression on his face, Marcus Tanner strode up to the center of the crowd.

"I was just back at the hotel," he announced gravely.

"Frank Wilson was supposed to be running the desk, but I didn't see him there. When I looked around, I found him doubled over on the floor. He had been stabbed a couple of times in the back."

Once again, the crowd began to buzz anxiously. Wearily, Sheriff Graham removed his hat and rubbed the back of his head.

"Who do you think might have done it?" he said in a quiet, meditative voice.

"You knew Wilson," Tanner replied sourly. "He didn't have an enemy in town."

"All right then, what about strangers?" the sheriff said, and started searching the crowd for unfamiliar faces. When he noticed Garrett standing off to the side with Layla and Dakota, his weathered features tightened.

"Know him?" he murmured to Tanner.

"Yeah, forget it," said the other. "He's all right. He was over at my place all night. You're going to have to come up with someone better than that."

"Listen, Tanner," Graham snapped, "you stay out of this. It's my job, so just leave it to me. Understand?"

Unsatisfied with their own speculations, the crowd began to barrage him with questions.

"Who could have killed them, sheriff?"

"Yeah, and why them?"

"What are you going to do about it, sheriff?"

"Hold on!" Jack Graham shouted heatedly. "The way I see it, there was only one killing tonight. Wilson's. The doc's was an accident. There's nothing in the way of evidence to say otherwise. All this happening on the same night is just a coincidence. A pretty bad one maybe, but that's all. Now all of you just go on home and let me do things my own way. This isn't the first time we've had trouble like this and it won't be the last."

Six

The Nightmare

Everything was suddenly out of balance. Dakota reeled backwards, falling helplessly through the air. He stumbled against a wall and slid to the ground. When he looked up, he saw a pair of dust-covered boots planted squarely beside his face. Someone was standing over him, laughing.

"Remember me, huh? Remember me?" a voice repeated over and over again.

A hollow shudder ran through Dakota. He knew who it was. Numbly, he tried to squirm around and reach for his gun. The dim awareness that he was not wearing his holster slowly came over him.

"Looking for this?"

The figure stooped down beside him and pressed a gun barrel to his head. Dakota saw a twisted eye, wide and unblinking, staring at him. He attempted to wrest his gaze from it, but could not. There was nowhere else to look.

"Hey, who's going to help you now?"

The gun barrel moved away slightly. The eye blinked, and Dakota had a sudden feeling of release. He glanced about. A heavy blanket of fog rose before him. He couldn't make out a thing.

"You're not going to find anything out there. Look here, look here. . . ."

The eye opened. Once again, Dakota felt its hypnotic pull. Powerless before it, he was drawn in. He knew he was flat on the ground, yet he seemed to be falling.

Set out clearly against a vast tract of wasteland, the way station came into view. And closer, beside the burnt rubble of a stagecoach, were Lavery and his men. Then

Dakota saw two other figures, a man and woman. Though their features were less distinct than those of the others, Dakota recognized the sad-eyed couple. Dead for more than five years, they were his parents.

"Take a good look. Those are the people you killed."

Dakota wanted to protest, but he could not move his lips. Willy swooped down on him and began to laugh. Dakota searched the mists, hoping to find Garrett. There was no one. The laughter grew louder, and Dakota realized that there were others besides Willy standing over him.

He saw Layla, dressed in her scant dance-hall costume, a merry smile dancing across her face. Behind her, crowded closely together, were the other saloon girls, all laughing. Dakota wrenched his face aside and saw Marta, hunched over, wearing black rags that scarcely covered her emaciated frame, slowly shuffling toward him. Her features were bathed in a strange red glow. Dakota wondered where the blood-tinged rays were coming from and saw that she was holding fire in her cupped hands.

"That's all. No more time for looking. You've seen all you're going to see."

The eye blinked and receded from view. The gun barrel swept through the air and pressed against Dakota's temple. Willy's grinning face appeared before him, and Dakota sank back impassively against the ground. He felt nothing, not even the desire to put up a fight.

There was a sharp burst of thunder. Dakota sprang up in bed. In a daze, he glanced about the small hotel room and gradually oriented himself to the unfamiliar surroundings.

"That sure was a good one," he told himself, much relieved, after he had caught his breath.

Another, more prolonged thunder roll shook the room. Dakota got out of bed and crossed over to the window. Drawing back the curtains, he found that his expectation of the previous few days had finally come to pass. The storm, always seeming to be just a few hours behind, had caught up with him. Rain was falling in a steady downpour, turning the streets to mud. It was impossible to tell what time of morning it was, for everything was overcast with a gloom so pervasive it made one wonder whether the sun had perhaps shifted from its course, never to return. Wrapped in a murky gray which only intermittent flashes of lightning could penetrate, sky and earth had become indistinguishable.

Dakota sighed and let the curtains fall back into place. He and Garrett would not be leaving town today.

He got back into bed and pulled the covers over him. He lay there for nearly a half hour in the semidarkness, fully awake, yet still troubling under the influence of the night's unrestful sleep. Finally, growing increasingly uneasy, he got up and dressed.

The lobby was empty when he came down the stairs. In a corner of the hall a large pendulum clock broke the silence with eight slow, resonant chimes. A short glance toward the unmanned lobby desk provided Dakota with a sharp reminder of the previous night's happenings. He turned and went outside.

He stopped at the edge of the porch, propped himself up against a post, and watched the storm. His gaze wandered past closed stores and empty streets, only occasionally catching sight of others who had ventured outdoors. Coming downstairs had done him little good. The town preferred to remain asleep on days like these; he was still alone. Lost in dreams, listening to the rain, he began pacing about.

He had reached the corner of the building when a flash of lightning briefly illuminated the small alleyway that ran between the hotel and the next row of stores. Something caught his eye and he stopped. Pressing close to the railing, he peered out and noticed what seemed like a bundle lying in the rain. In the dismal light it took him a few moments to distinguish its features, but when he did his expression altered sharply. He swung over the railing and ran.

Barely conscious of the storm, he stopped in the center of the narrow alley and knelt hurriedly beside the unstirring body. His red-stained clothing drenched through, the man looked as though he might have been there, facedown in the mud, for hours. In his back were four knife slashes. Dakota turned him over to look at the face, saw death's pale, frozen expression and instantly looked away. He got to his feet, shaken, not knowing what to do first.

And then he glimpsed, further down the alley, the rain-obscured outlines of a man. Dakota went numb, it suddenly seeming to him as though he were once again being plunged into his nightmare. He darted for the side of the building and waited. But the hazy figure merely stood there, silent, watching. Dakota called out, but received no response. He huddled closer to the wall and remained as immobile as the other. Finally, seeking release in some form of action, he drew his gun and marched cautiously forward. When he reached the alley's end and saw his fancied opponent, standing upright a few feet from a carpenter's shed, Dakota felt a twinge of disgust—for himself and the entire situation.

It was a coffin.

Cursing his imagination—which, along with his dreams, was in fact closer to the truth than he could ever have thought—he dashed back up the alley, past the corpse, not stopping until he found his way to the sheriff's office.

Jack Graham was sitting with his feet up on the desk, a mug of coffee in his hands, quietly pondering the murder of Frank Wilson, when Dakota stepped in the door.

"Sheriff," said the youth, "there's been some more trouble. Down the street. Someone else has been stabbed."

"What?" Graham exploded, and was already on his feet. "Who is it?"

"I don't know. He looked like a cowhand, but I can't say for sure." Dakota paused to catch his breath and then added, "He's dead, sheriff."

The sheriff slammed his coffee down on the desk and grabbed his coat from the chair. "Come on," he snapped abruptly. "Show me."

Like Dakota before him, Jack Graham stopped short at the sight of the body. Slowly, burning with rancor, he crouched down and examined the mud-clotted face.

"Goddamn. . . ." he murmured under his breath.

"Do you know him?" asked Dakota.

"Yeah, he worked out on one of the spreads near here. Played cards with him a couple of times." He looked up. "Give me a hand and let's get him out of the rain."

They trudged back with the corpse to Graham's office

and laid it down on the floor of one of the cells. Graham contemplated the ranch hand with a bitter look, then threw a blanket over him and motioned Dakota into the front room.

"Want some coffee? Bet you can use it."

"Thanks," Dakota nodded. He followed Graham to the stove and began warming himself by the fire.

"Do you have any idea who might have done it?" he asked quietly, breaking a brief silence.

"No, can't say I do." Graham glanced up from the coffeepot. "Do you?"

"Me? What do you mean?"

"Well, let's put it like this," the sheriff drawled in a tone that made Dakota uneasy, "I've got two men who've been killed outright and another no one knows about one way or the other. Now I've got to start looking for this killer somewhere, right? So it might as well be with you."

He handed Dakota a mug of coffee and flashed an unsettling smile. "For beginners," he went on, "would you mind telling me what you were doing out there in the first place when you found him?"

"I wasn't doing anything," the youth replied nervously. "I was just walking around."

"In the rain, huh?"

"No, I—" Dakota stopped and tried to collect himself. "Listen, sheriff, I didn't kill that man. If I had, do you think I would have come over here to tell you about it?"

Graham gave him a hard, penetrating look.

"Okay," he said finally, the wrinkles that had formed at the corners of his eyes beginning to disappear. "Forget it. I reckon you're a little young for that sort of thing anyway. Come on over and sit down."

Graham strode across the room and kicked a chair over beside his desk. "I'll tell you, it's reached a point I don't know who to trust anymore," he said by way of explanation as he dropped wearily into his seat. "I've been up half the night trying to sort things out, and right around now I'm ready to start springing at just about anybody."

"I can understand that," Dakota said, growing more relaxed. "And what with this second one, I guess it doesn't make things any easier."

"Nope, it sure doesn't," Graham echoed grimly. He

sank back and brooded over his coffee. The steady throbbing of the rain filled the room.

"The way I see it," he mused aloud, "since there isn't anything else to go on, the first problem is to figure out whether the killer is someone from here in town or just some stranger who's passing through."

"Which do you think it is?"

"Well, let's start by saying it's a stranger," he said, once again running through the process of deliberation he had repeated over and over to himself through the night. "From there we have another question: why would a person kill someone he doesn't know?"

"For money, I suppose," said Dakota. "That's usually the reason, isn't it?"

"Right—except Wilson had all his money on him when we found him at the hotel. And as for that one in there," Graham added with a glance toward the cells, "I'd bet he didn't have the price of a drink on him by the time he left the Scarlet Palace last night. No one would have killed *him* for his money."

The sheriff took another sip of coffee, then continued, "All right, since it wasn't for money, I'll go on and suppose that the killer had some sort of grudge against these people. But in that case, it can't be anyone who's just passing through. A person can't hold a grudge against someone he doesn't know. He'd have to be plumb out of his mind to want to kill someone he hasn't even met before."

"Then you think it's one of the people from around here?"

"Well, I'm not sure what else to think. There aren't all that many other choices. And anyway, we don't get a whole lot of people passing through in the first place."

Graham tilted back his chair and made himself more comfortable. After so many hours alone, it was a relief to have someone he could speak with. It helped clear his mind on a number of problems.

"Here, let me tell you about this town I was thinking about before," he said. "Maybe it'll make more sense out of all this. I heard about it from someone else, but it strikes me as just crazy enough to make me sure the story's true.

"Every time they had any trouble, the people who lived

86

in this place had the habit of going and locking up the first stranger they could find. One time, when a rancher and his whole family were found murdered, they got a hold of some poor drifter and strung him up. They were so sure they had the right one they didn't even bother asking any questions. Well, it was too bad for them they didn't, because a couple of days later another family was killed, just the same way as the first. So what did they do after that, you ask? Don't think they got any smarter. They did the same thing they were used to doing all along. They went and lynched some other stranger all over again.

"You know, close to twenty people in all were killed before they found out who did it. And it turned out it was someone they'd known all their lives, someone who'd gotten it into his head that he wanted more land—his neighbors' land. They were so busy hunting strangers they never thought of looking for one of their own. That was the last thing they wanted to believe, that it could be one of their own."

"But in this case it isn't land," said Dakota.

"No, it isn't. But who knows what's going on in the minds of those people out there. It could even be less of a reason than land. That wouldn't make any difference."

The sheriff sank back and pondered the enormity of the situation, the grotesqueness of whatever motives might be involved. He heaved a deep sigh of disgust.

"It's funny," he then said, his train of thought beginning to solidify into a theory, "but in a way I've been like the people of that other town. Like before, when I started asking you all those questions. And last night, after the fire, the first thing I did was to start looking for strangers. I saw one person I didn't know and right off . . . Hey," he interrupted himself as he remembered his suspicions regarding Garrett, "weren't you with him? And there was a woman there too?"

Dakota nodded. "We noticed how you were looking at us."

Graham, too, began to smile. His strong, sharply cast features were not given to betraying signs of emotion, but he was starting to see a good bit of himself in this youth sitting opposite him.

"Well, that just goes to show you," he said. "I reckon I sort of owe you both an apology."

"Forget it," Dakota said with a shrug. "It doesn't make any difference. There's no harm in asking questions."

"No, I guess not. It's when the questions stop and the lynchings begin that you've got your real trouble. And that's something I'm not about to let happen around here." His expression was filled with a deep-set resolve. A loner for most of his life, he had at bottom little trust for the townspeople. He was certain that, given their way, they would sooner or later be marching down the streets in an angry mob.

Graham rose heavily from his seat and picked up the metal coffee mug. "Want some more?" he asked.

"Sure," Dakota said, and followed him to the stove. Like the sheriff, he was glad to have the opportunity to talk. Their conversation had already done much to dispel the lingering effects of his dreams.

"So what do you think you're going to do?" he asked as Graham poured out a fresh round of coffee.

"Well, boy, I don't rightly know," said the other. "That's what everyone else around here has been asking me, and they don't really like it when I don't have any simple answers to give them. They figure I'm the law, so somehow I should know more than they do. They don't like hearing that none of this makes any more sense to me than it does to them. In the end they don't care what I do, so long as I'm doing something."

"But what about your idea that it's one of them? Isn't that something to work with?"

"Not really," Jack Graham replied with a sour smile. "Not until someone's caught doing it. I can't exactly go around and start questioning each and every one of them. They'd like that less than anything else. Like I said before, the last thing they'd want to believe is that it's one of them."

"But you do think it is one of them."

"Well, that's what everything seems to lead up to. But that doesn't help one way or the other. I don't mind admitting, boy, it's a mess, a real mess. On one side I've got a bunch of murders on my hands, and on the other I've got a lot of angry people who want something done about

88

it. And I'm right there in the middle—not the best place to be when something like this is going on."

"No, it doesn't sound it," agreed Dakota.

"Well, it isn't, take it from me," the sheriff answered grimly. "And in all this only one other thing's for certain—it's going to take more than a badge and a gun to figure out what's going on around here. A lot more."

He was interrupted at this point by a heavy-set man who came bolting in through the door. His rain-soaked face contorted with fear, he exclaimed between panting breaths:

"Sheriff, you'd better come quick! There's been another murder!"

Seven

For the Sake
of Murder

They found Bill Johnson sprawled behind the counter of his general store, gaping knife wounds in his back. The small, white-haired man must have been caught by surprise, for there were no signs of a struggle. Nor was there any indication of what the intruder could possibly have wanted. Everything, including the cash register and gun racks, seemed to have been left untouched.

Lou Gardner, the dead storekeeper's oversized assistant, explained that Johnson had planned to work late the night before to bring some of his orders up to date, but had little else to add. He had left at the usual time the previous evening and not returned to the store until just a few minutes ago. When the sheriff asked him if he could tell whether anything was missing, the hulking, slow-witted man gave a helpless shrug of his shoulders. Nervous, badly shaken, he offered to check the inventory, but Graham told him to go home and relax instead; it probably wouldn't help anyway.

Graham had a look around for himself, but gave up finally in disgust. Johnson, too, appeared to have been killed a good number of hours before, and in the same manner as the other victims, but besides the most obvious of observations, there was no explaining what all the men could have had in common.

With the help of Dakota and Gardner, the sheriff brought the body back to the jail and set it down beside the unstirring ranch hand. Then, having little else he could do, Graham set out to patrol the dismal streets, hoping to be nearby the next time something was about to happen—and hoping as well not to encounter any more corpses along the way.

Dakota accompanied him for the start of the rounds, but on the sheriff's suggestion, went indoors when they reached the hotel. The youth remained for a while on the porch and watched the solitary figure disappear into the rain. He then went upstairs, to Garrett's room. He knocked, but instead of a response, he heard a pair of laughing voices coming from behind him. He crossed the hall, listened with curiosity, then rapped softly on Layla's door.

"Well there you are," the dark-eyed women said in cheery greeting. "Come on in."

Although they both seemed glad to see him, Dakota nonetheless felt as though he were intruding. The sight of Garrett, who was seated comfortably in a chair near the bed, made the youth feel even more ill at ease. The entire situation had for him an odd, dreamy quality. His experiences of the past two hours had left their mark on him. He looked at them strangely, as if he were just wakened, unable to see what reason they could have had for being in such high spirits.

"Where have you been?" Layla asked, noticing his rain-soaked clothing.

"Outside," Dakota said quietly.

"Outside?" said Garrett. "I was over at your room before, but when you didn't answer I thought you were still sleeping."

"No, I wasn't sleeping," Dakota answered, and began relating to them what had happened. The smiles quickly dropped from Garrett and Layla's faces.

"So that makes it four deaths in one night," Garrett observed in a steely tone when Dakota had finished.

"And there may be some more before this is over," Layla added.

"Why? What do you mean?" Dakota asked, eager to get their opinions on the subject.

"Well, I hope I'm wrong, but from the sound of it I don't think I am," Layla replied. "I've seen this sort of thing happen before, and if it's the same as what's going on here, then I'd say this town's going to be in for its share of trouble for a while."

"But what kind of trouble? That's just what I don't understand. None of this makes any sense."

"And that's just the kind of trouble I'm talking about. The kind that doesn't make any sense. This wouldn't be the first time that someone's gone out and killed people for no other reason than that he likes the sight of blood."

"But that's crazy!" cried Dakota. "A person would have to be crazy to do something like that!"

"Maybe so, Dakota," Garrett put in, "but that's what senseless murders are. They don't have anything to do with the reasons you'd normally think of. It's murder for the sake of murder—nothing more than that. Someone gets it into his head to start destroying everything and everyone around him, and that's just what he does."

The man's words produced a sudden, empty twinge in the pit of Dakota's stomach. But the sensation disappeared before he could put a name on it, his thoughts quickly went on to other things, and it was forgotten for the time being.

"But wouldn't it be easy to find out who's doing it?" he asked. "Wouldn't he just be running through the streets killing people?"

"Have you seen anyone doing that?" answered the woman.

"No," he sighed. "But it would sure make it a whole lot easier to catch him."

"That's the trouble. There's no telling who it is. It could be anyone, anyone at all."

Dakota compared what they said with what the sheriff had told him earlier and realized that it all amounted to the same thing: there was nothing whatsoever that could be relied upon as certain.

"And this is what you think's happening here?" he asked. He wanted to hear something, anything, that would give him some small measure of reassurance.

"Well, like I said before, I could be wrong," Layla answered. "There's no saying for sure one way or the other."

Dakota looked to Garrett, but the man had nothing to add.

"Okay," he then said, "let's say you're right. Then

92

wouldn't you want to get out of town as quickly as possible? If there isn't any reason behind all this, then you could get killed as easily as anyone else."

Layla smiled. "And as easily here as anywhere else. You let me know about a place where everything's safe and secure, and I'll pack my bags and go there right now. Until then, I'll just stay here and do the best I can to keep myself out of trouble."

"And where would you go?" Garrett asked him. "You know that nothing's guaranteed for sure, no matter where you find yourself."

"I guess so," the youth muttered gloomily, wishing he could believe otherwise. "I guess so."

But Dakota was unable to let matters stand at that. He could accept that there was nothing comforting to be found in the entire situation, but not that it was all haphazard, without meaning. He struggled over and over with the same thoughts, trying to extract an ounce of sense from a series of events which had seemingly little to offer in the way of intelligibility.

And then he hit upon something. It was not with any measure of certainty that he reached his conclusion, nor through any logical process of thought. Neither applied here. It was instead something he felt, or, to be more precise, something he was just beginning to feel. Because of the inexactness of these dim glimmerings of a hypothesis, Dakota at first hesitated before relating it to Garrett and Layla. But finally, as the sheriff had done with him earlier, he decided to tell them, if for no other reason than to hear how it would sound when spoken aloud.

They were in the Scarlet Palace Saloon, at a table near the front windows, watching the steady downpour of rain outside. Gathered about them at the bar and in various corners of the spacious room were small clusters of townspeople who, like them, had found themselves with little else to do until there came a letup in the weather. But for most of these citizens of New Eden it was also something more than the weather. They were uneasy, and had come here to pass the slow afternoon hours in the company of friends. The same topic of conversation could be heard wherever one turned. Each of them took a turn at offering an explanation for the murders, but not once did they hit upon anything that met with the satisfaction of their listeners.

"They're not going to give up, are they?" Garrett remarked when the conversation from a nearby table became a little more animated than usual.

Layla glanced in their direction. Seated in the center of the group of nervous shopkeepers were Marcus Tanner and Jason Pratt.

"Oh, I guess it makes them feel a little better about things," she said with a sigh.

Dakota saw his opportunity. "Well, if it'll make either of *you* feel any better, I've come up with an idea myself," he said, deciding it would be best, considering the mood Garrett and Layla were in, if he broached the subject lightheartedly. "At least it's a little different than what they're saying."

The man and woman gave him a look, but said nothing to encourage him.

"Well . . ." Dakota said, hesitating a moment before plunging ahead, "you remember that cross-eyed kid Willy from yesterday, don't you? The one who got away? Well, what if he followed us here and—"

"You think he's the one who killed those people?" Layla interrupted.

"Why? Isn't it possible?"

"It's possible, Dakota, but it isn't very probable," she said with a patient smile.

"But why not? He'd want revenge for what we did, wouldn't he?"

"Exactly. That's just the point," Layla retorted matter-of-factly. "If it *was* him, why would he bother with those other people? Wouldn't we be the ones he'd want to take his revenge out on? He'd be trying to kill us, not them."

"And there's one more thing," said Garrett. "I had him on my mind yesterday, while we were riding here. I didn't like the idea that he might want vengeance for what had happened, so I kept an eye out for him, just on the odd chance that he might be following us. And if he was, I would have seen him. He didn't know where we were going, so he would have had to stay close enough behind to keep us in sight—in which case I would have noticed him sooner or later. I think you know that. So I'd say there isn't much of a chance it's him."

Dakota stopped, not knowing how to answer him. Their arguments seemed conclusive enough, but he was not convinced. The feeling was still there. He turned to Layla and protested, "But you said before that it could be anyone."

"But that doesn't include people who couldn't possibly be here in the first place, does it? Think about it a minute. If he were here in town, don't you think someone would have noticed him by now? He didn't exactly have the kind of face you'd forget all that easily."

Dakota replied with a slow, thoughtful nod.

"Like I told you, Dakota," Garrett said evenly, "I also thought it might be him for a while. But when I couldn't find anything to support it, I decided it was just that—a thought, and nothing else. Now if you want to believe it, go ahead. But I don't think it's too good an idea to get carried away by your imagination, especially with something like this. You end up fighting things that aren't even there, and it doesn't help."

"Okay, I suppose you're right," sighed the youth.

The man and woman made a few last disheartening comments on the situation, then dropped the topic altogether. Sober, introspective, they once again turned their attention to the falling rain. Dakota tried repeatedly in the ensuing silence to accommodate himself to their suggestions, but could not shake a lingering feeling of dissatisfaction. Finally, growing increasingly restless, he excused himself and rose from the table.

"Where are you going?" asked Garrett.

"Outside. I just want to get some air," Dakota said, and walked off.

Layla had little difficulty in seeing what was the matter. "I don't think he's taking all this very well," she told Garrett. "It's beginning to get to him."

"Yeah, I know the feeling," Garrett said with a maudlin smile. His eyes remained on the doors for a moment after Dakota had gone out. "It's not easy those first couple of times when you begin to realize that things don't always fit together perfectly."

"And when people don't start making all that much

sense either?" Layla offered as a conclusion to a long-familiar feeling.

Garrett nodded. "That too, that too."

Unable to be more in agreement, they fell silent. Their eyes met, and they both knew that, for them, everything suddenly did fit.

"Maybe you ought to go outside with him," Layla suggested quietly. "He could probably use you."

"I'm not sure I'd be of much help," Garrett said, a deep part of him not wanting to go anywhere at that moment. "Everyone has to go through it sooner or later. Sometimes it's better to leave a person alone so he can make his own peace with things."

"But maybe this isn't one of those times," answered Layla. "Seeing you in here with me can't make things any easier for him."

"What do you mean?"

The woman looked at him. "I think you know what I mean."

Garrett smiled. "And is he wrong for seeing us like that?"

"No," she replied, "I don't think so. But we can always talk about that later."

"Okay, okay," Garrett said, laughing softly. The promise of a rain check would keep him for now. He went after the youth and found him standing gloomily by the corner of the porch.

"What's the matter, boy? You still thinking about it?"

"I heard everything you told me before, but I just can't get him out of my mind," Dakota said, the words pouring out. "I just can't."

"Nothing we said made any difference?"

"No, not really. It should have, I know, but it didn't."

"All right," responded the man. "Then what are you going to do about it?"

"What *can* I do about it? Where am I supposed to go? I don't even know if I'm right."

"Well, I'm not saying I agree with you, because you know I don't. But if I were in your place and felt the way you did, I'd go and tell the sheriff about it."

"But what good will that do?"

"It would be better than just sitting in there like those

people and talking about it all day. At least you'd be doing something, for whatever it's worth. It's the sheriff who's trying to find this killer, so more than anyone else, he's the one who ought to know what you think. It would then be up to him to decide what he wants to make of it."

"Why should I go to him though?" Dakota said in exasperation. "*You* don't even think I'm right."

"Look, Dakota, I don't have any book with all the answers. There's never any saying who's right or wrong until it's already done and finished with. Up to then you're just going to have to go ahead and do what you think's best. Even if it turns out you're wrong in the end. That's all any man can do—unless he'd rather sit around and worry until everything's over. But I don't think that's you."

Dakota's face brightened slightly.

"I think I'm going to stay out here a little while longer, okay?" he said after a short pause.

"Sure," Garrett smiled. "See you inside."

But Dakota called him as he was turning to go. "Garrett? If I wanted to leave town, would you be willing to go also?"

"You know I'm not much on running away from things, Dakota," replied the man. "I think it would be better for you to stay and see how it all turns out."

"Is it that, or does Layla have something to do with it?"

Garrett had expected the question sooner or later, but had no ready answer to offer. "Well, let's just say we're *both* staying to see how it all turns out, all right?"

Dakota would have liked to hear something more reassuring, but realized that there was not much else to be said. Everything, including this, seemed to be a question mark, which, for the time being at least, was not about to yield any ready solutions. He met the man's gaze and nodded.

"All right."

For a second time that day, Dakota found himself leaning up against the porch railing, alone with his thoughts. But this time there was a difference. Garrett had helped him to see that he could no longer straddle the fence, continually disturbed by dreams and fears. He had to do something about what he felt or forget it altogether. And

97

the knowledge that there was a choice to be made filled him with a sense of strength and well-being.

Dakota held his hand out to the rain and toyed absently with the runoff from the eaves. For long minutes passing, he tried to sift everything through his mind and put it all into place. As had happened many times before, however, he found that all the logical trains of thought led him nowhere. The arguments were once again coming to a dead standstill. It was then that he noticed a tall man in a slicker coming up the walk across the way. Dakota recognized the sheriff's unhurried gait.

And his decision was made.

Eight

Two Possibilities

Jack Graham got up from his desk and began pacing the room. "I think I'm going to have to agree with your friends," he decided finally. "It doesn't sound very likely to me."

Dakota regarded him with a slightly wearied expression, but said nothing. He had no desire to push the matter any further. There was, after all, little reason for the sheriff to have reacted differently.

"Tell me, Dakota," the man went on, curious to understand why Dakota had come to him with his story, "what makes you think you're right?"

"Nothing," the youth said stolidly. "Nothing at all. It's just a feeling I have."

"A feeling, hmm?" Graham repeated blandly, wishing Dakota would have given him something more substantial to work with. "Well, you were right to want to tell me about it. I appreciate it, and I'll keep it in mind. Maybe it'll be of some help."

"That's not the only reason I wanted to talk with you," Dakota interrupted in a steady voice. He continued, without waiting for a response, "I don't think it would be a good idea for you to try to catch the killer alone, sheriff. If you remember, you yourself said it could be anyone out there. And if that's true, it's going to take more than one person to find him."

"And you want to help?"

"That's right," Dakota replied with a short nod. Something had changed markedly in his manner. The hesitancy of before had vanished; he was more direct, self-assured.

He no longer wanted to get involved in drawn-out discussions. No one had any real solutions to offer anyway. The time had come for him to start turning his energies in a more useful direction.

"Do you know what you're asking to get yourself into? Whoever it is out there, he's not playing around. You saw what he did."

"I can take care of myself." For emphasis, Dakota pulled back his jacket and displayed the six-gun holstered at his side.

"You know how to use that?"

"I wouldn't advise him to try coming at me with that knife of his. He'd never get the chance to use it."

Graham could see he wasn't boasting. Dakota had told him a little about himself earlier, and the glimpses Graham got were sufficient for him to draw a few conclusions of his own. He knew from past experience the kind of life Dakota must have led in his years of roaming from place to place with Garrett. He therefore had little difficulty in believing that Dakota could handle himself—better, in all probability, than most of the sheltered citizens of New Eden.

"Did you ask your friend Garrett what he has to say about this?" he asked, still not entirely convinced.

"No, I didn't," Dakota said evenly. "But I don't have to. I'm old enough. He trusts me to do what I think's right."

And with good reason, Graham thought, smiling to himself.

"But there's one thing I still don't understand," he said after some further deliberation. "What do you want to get involved in this whole business for? You know, you could end up getting hurt, maybe even killed. And what for? You can get out of town any time you want. None of this has anything to do with you."

"But maybe it does, sheriff," responded Dakota. "Maybe it does."

"And how's that?"

"It could always turn out that my guess about the killer was right. It might be a small chance, but it's still a chance. There's no saying for sure one way or the other, but if I *am* right, then this is more my fight than anyone else's."

100

"And if you're wrong?"

"In that case, I'd just be helping to do a job that's got to be done. But, either way, I can't sit still and do nothing. Not as long as there is that chance that it *is* my fight."

Jack Graham dropped his eyes and strode meditatively across the room. He stopped at the window and looked out on the rainy streets of the town he had chosen to call home. He had often regretted that choice, for, instead of finding the kind of life he had hoped for, he had been left even more isolated than he was previously, when he led a drifter's existence. And his job was the reason. In the eyes of the townspeople, he was the embodiment of the law, but little else. They left him alone to do the job they had neither the desire nor the courage to perform themselves, gave him the measure of respect due his position, but otherwise steered clear of him, shutting him out from their daily lives. As far as they were concerned, he was a man of violence, having more in common with the gunmen he was hired to bring to justice than he did with any of them.

He had seen this attitude repeatedly during the morning, when he had made the rounds of the townspeople's homes, trying to gather what information he could about the murders. His attempts at finding clues had turned out to be of no value at all. Fearful of somehow being implicated, they told him as little as possible, and seemed relieved when he was about to go. The last thing they wanted was to become involved, and as a result had little to offer in the way of help. They all appeared to him equally innocent, equally guilty. He was left just where he had started.

And now, as he was considering what to do, Graham realized that there was not one person among the peace-loving citizens of New Eden whom he could say he knew really well. The thought irritated him, all the more so since he could not, even had he wanted to, look to any of them for help. In many respects they were all strangers— and, consequently, all possible suspects. Never seeking his friendship, not one of them had ever earned his trust.

He turned from the window. Dakota's eyes were flashing brightly; they peered deeply into the sheriff's.

"All right, son," Jack Graham said at last. "It looks like you've got yourself a job."

The Scarlet Palace Saloon saw more business that day than it had in many a previous afternoon. One after another, the town's idle shopkeepers came drifting in out of the rain to find a willing ear. The room became filled with the sound of their ceaseless conjectures.

From all the numerous arguments there was, however, one point of agreement which did gradually seem to emerge: regardless of who was committing them, the murders weren't going to do the town's trade one bit of good at all. The word would spread; there was no stopping it. People would stay clear of New Eden until their troubles were over.

Like many others there, Marcus Tanner was made particularly anxious by this aspect of the situation. Before making the westward move, he and his partner had tried to think of everything to insure the success of their long-held dream, but they had never taken problems such as this into account. They had often heard tales about the roughness of life in the West, but it had somehow always sounded exciting to them. They had no way of knowing beforehand the effect it might have on a frontier town. To be certain, there was crime back East, but it never reached such violent extremes; it always seemed to remain within the control of the police. There could be a murder down the street, but it would not affect your life, and certainly not your business. Whatever might happen, you could always expect to go on as before.

But he had reached certain different conclusions in the years since coming to New Eden. It was sometimes necessary, he now believed, for everyone to take on the responsibility of protecting the laws. It was the least any good citizen could do, especially at a time when the sheriff wasn't managing too well on his own. And this certainly seemed to be one of those times.

Marcus Tanner got up from where he had been sitting, climbed atop the bar, and called for everyone to gather around him. The shopkeepers had a strong liking for Tanner. Handsome, well-educated, wealthier than they, he was their natural leader. And the fact that he, along with his less conspicuous partner, had given them this palace of entertainment did much to increase his popularity with them. In addition to providing them with a taste of big-city luxury, the saloon had brought the town a good deal of extra business, and they were not the sort to forget this. They clustered about the bar, eager to hear what Tanner would have to tell them.

Seated by their table at the window, Garrett and Layla interrupted their own, more personal conversation to listen as Tanner began addressing the small crowd. But the man and woman quickly lost all patience with Tanner's patronizing remarks, and exchanged a look of bored desperation.

"Want to leave?" Garrett asked. Layla gave a short, decisive nod.

It was then that the sheriff, with Dakota at his side, came in. They had heard the noisy gathering from down the street.

"Hold on," said Layla. Tanner had just launched into a discourse on the townspeople's collective duty to help keep the peace. She slipped back into her chair to await the confrontation. "This could turn out to be interesting."

"The way I see it," Tanner was saying, "we all have a stake in this. So it's up to us to make sure it doesn't happen again."

"Hold it right there, Tanner," the sheriff interrupted. "It's not up to you people to do anything. No one around here's going to take the law into his own hands, unless he wants to have me to deal with."

The crowd receded slightly at his approach.

"And what would you suggest we do, sheriff?" Tanner retorted. "Just sit back and watch?"

"Well, if it's suggestions you're looking for, I've got a couple," Graham said dryly. "For a start, stay out of this—all of you. Take my word for it, your help isn't going to make things any easier."

"You're going to try to find that killer by yourself?" asked Tanner.

"No, not exactly. I've got one person to help me, and that should be enough." The sheriff's gaze moved to Dakota.

"Him?" one of the storekeepers called in disbelief. "You can't be serious, sheriff. Don't you think he's a little young?"

103

Dakota regarded the crowd impassively. He had long ago learned from Garrett the art of remaining unprovoked. But as he listened to their protests, none of which they would have dared to speak had they not had the safety of numbers, he began to understand why the sheriff hadn't the slightest trust in any of them.

"Now listen!" Jack Graham growled at them. "He's going to be helping me, and that's all there is to it. He knows it's going to be dangerous, but he still wants to help. That's good enough for me, and it should be good enough for all of you. So if I were you, I'd think twice before making fun of him. He's got courage and that's—" He stopped himself short before saying what he really felt about them. "—well, that's a good thing to have."

"All right, sheriff, all right," Tanner said haughtily, thinking everyone was still solidly behind him. "But what about the rest of us? Or are we too old?"

"Look, Tanner, I don't want to see anyone else get killed any more than you do," Graham replied in a more restrained tone as he tried to reason with him. "And I'm doing my best to make sure that doesn't happen. But if all of you are out there roaming around the streets, it'll just give the killer more targets to aim at. Sure I could use your help. But it isn't worth the risk."

The sheriff had chosen the right approach. Confronted with the possibility of putting their own lives in danger, the townspeople grew somewhat more subdued.

"Okay, sheriff, then what do you suggest we do?" one of them asked, suddenly respectful.

"Well, the best thing you could do is to stay indoors. Don't go outside tonight unless you absolutely have to. That'll cut down the chances of anything happening to you. Not only that, it'll make my job easier for me. The fewer people out on the streets, the better. That will give me fewer of you to worry about, and it'll also make it that much simpler for me to spot anyone who's doing something suspicious."

"Next off, you're going to be telling me to close down," Tanner said bitterly. He could see he was losing his sway over the crowd, and was not about to give it up that easily.

"I'm not going to waste my time telling you to do anything, Tanner. That's up to you. But if I were the rest of you, I'd stay home with my wife and kids. They're going to need you more than I will, and that's where you'll be safest."

"Tell us, sheriff," the saloon owner once again broke in, "do you have any idea yet who the murderer is?"

"Yeah, I've got it boiled down to two possibilities," Graham said with a sarcastic smile. "It's either someone who's keeping very quiet or someone who's making a hell of a lot more noise than he should."

"And what do you mean by that?"

The sheriff gave him an icy stare. "Think about it."

Garrett and Layla shared a quiet chuckle. They were glad they had stayed around. It had certainly proved to be an interesting spectacle.

"One other thing, sheriff," Tanner said, still not about to yield. "While all of us are busy locking ourselves indoors, what are you going to be doing?"

"Leave that to me, Tanner. Okay?"

"Sure, sure. But let me just tell you this: if there's one more death—just one more—we won't be leaving it to you."

"Don't threaten me," Graham said in a low, steely voice. "I don't like it."

"I'm not threatening you," the other replied innocently, filled with his sense of citizen's duty. "I'm just saying what I think will be best for the town as a whole."

"Why don't you save your speeches for Election Day? They'll be worth more then." Like the youth standing beside him, Graham knew something about the uselessness of succumbing to provocation.

He was about to leave, when Dakota quietly reminded him of something, and he turned. "By the way," he asked, "have any of you seen a cross-eyed kid, about fifteen or sixteen, anywhere around?"

Dakota pursed his lips disappointedly as he surveyed the roomful of blank stares and shaking heads.

"Okay, forget it. It's nothing important." Graham looked at Dakota and made an empty gesture with his hands. Dakota smiled weakly and tried to shrug it off. With a glance in Garrett and Layla's direction, he followed the sheriff out of the saloon.

Everyone seemed to decide at once that the meeting had come to an end. More concerned with personal strategies than with any collective action, they returned to their tables to discuss the matter of their safety among themselves. Marcus Tanner was left standing atop the bar without an audience.

"What do we do now?" Dakota asked when he and the sheriff stepped out onto the porch.

"Well, I don't know about you, but I'm going to go get myself a little sleep," the tall man replied. "I could sure do with some, and I'd suggest you do the same. We may have ourselves a long night ahead of us."

"But shouldn't we be keeping an eye on things just in case something happens?"

"I wouldn't worry about that too much," said Graham. "So far all the murders have taken place at night, and it's my guess that we'd be better off if we spent our time resting up for later. Right now there are too many people around. The killer probably won't make another move until after nightfall—if he's going to make one at all."

"You think there's a chance he won't?"

"Who can say? By now he's got to know that we're going to be watching for him. He might just decide to sit back and wait for a better time. What does he have to lose? He knows that we don't have any idea who he is. For all we know, he could have been right there in the saloon, laughing at everything that was going on."

"Well, all I can say is I hope you're wrong. I'd be a lot happier if he tried something tonight, so we can get all this over with."

"So would I, boy, so would I. But I guess we'll find out later, won't we?" the sheriff replied with a bleak smile. Starting down from the porch, he told Dakota to come over to his office in an hour or two, and walked off into the rain.

Dakota stood there a moment longer, wondering whether the sheriff had been right, whether the murderer was, perhaps, one of the townspeople. When he turned, he found Garrett calmly standing behind him at the saloon doors. He stopped short, his face flushing with nervous anticipation. He braced himself for what the man might have to say about his actions.

"So you decided to do somthing about those feelings of yours," Garrett wryly commented.

"I had to do it," Dakota said quickly in his defense. "Don't you see? If it is Willy, then all this is my fault. If I'd only been able to shoot him yesterday, none of this would have happened."

"Don't be that hard on yourself. The past is over and done with. You should now be concentrating on the job you've got ahead of you."

"Then you don't mind that I'm doing this?"

"No. I might not particularly agree with you, but I don't mind."

"Are you sure?" Dakota asked cautiously, his eyes beginning to brighten.

Garrett smiled. "I'm sure. Everyone's got to start cutting his own path through life sooner or later, and it looks like that time's come for you. And I'm happy to see it. It's a good sign."

Regarding him with a father's warmth, Garrett came closer and put his hand on the youth's shoulder. "Just be careful, Dakota, all right? I'm not going to be out here with you on these streets tonight because ... well, that's just the way it's going to have to be. This is something you have to see through for yourself. But I just wanted you to know that I'll be around if you need me. Tonight or any other time, don't ever be ashamed to ask me for help if you need it. Remember, I already know that you're able to take care of yourself. I know it very well."

"Thanks, Garrett," Dakota said quietly, holding back his swelling emotions.

Garrett looked at him deeply, gave his arm an affectionate squeeze, and started to go back inside.

"You'll be with Layla?" asked Dakota.

The man turned and nodded.

"You like her, don't you?"

"I suppose you can say that," answered Garrett. Then, noticing Dakota's slightly downcast expression, "Now I guess it's my turn to ask if *you* mind."

"No," Dakota said, attempting a brave smile. "No more than you did."

"I'm glad to hear you say that," Garrett replied. Giving

107

a short wink that expressed everything he had left unsaid, he went into the saloon.

But Dakota's smile vanished as the doors swung emptily back into place. He tried repeating to himself Garrett's words of encouragement, but they did little to relieve the feelings of loneliness that were gnawing at him. Yes, he was getting older, and maybe that was why he was beginning to feel this new sense of responsibility. But that path Garrett had mentioned before, that was what bothered him most. He was just starting to understand what would be involved in the double task of clearing and traveling such a path, and the prospect seemed more difficult than he had ever imagined before—and more lonely as well. To make matters even worse, he hadn't the slightest idea where it would all lead him anyway.

And then he reached the culmination of his bleak reflections. More than ever before, he was struck by the realization that he and Garrett might someday have to travel separate ways. If it wasn't Layla, if it wasn't these murders, then there could always be something else to come between them. Suddenly, feeling the deadening pull of a vast emptiness, he broke free of these thoughts. Of all the various possibilities he was wrestling with, this was the last one he wanted to confront.

He closed his eyes, exhausted by his efforts at solving problems which only the future could answer. A heavy languor overcame him. He attempted to think of something he could do to distract himself, but was caught fast in the dulling hold of an all-encompassing lethargy. He simply stood there, yielding before the overpowering reality of the moment—a moment when everything had suddenly become foreign, uncaring, uncertain.

For lack of a better solution, he decided to follow the sheriff's suggestion and try to get some sleep. Perhaps this alone could grant him some relief. He went up to his room and dropped listlessly onto the bed. With less effort than he expected, he managed to clear his mind, but, too alert for sleep, his attention began to center instead on a collection of disturbing sounds that seemed to rise all around him. From downstairs, he heard the babbling of voices from the saloon. And from the room directly above his own, there was the slow thudding of someone restlessly pacing around. He tried everything to block the noises out, even throwing a pillow over his head, but only ended by focusing on them all the more. In disgust, he passed the time wondering, as he had many times before, how people could ever tolerate the notion of settling down in towns, where everyone seemed to be living on top of one other, where you couldn't sneeze without having someone hear.

For nearly an hour he lay on top of the covers, fully dressed except for his boots, neither asleep nor completely awake. Then his eyes opened; he sat up. Gradually, he became aware that something had changed. The noises had stopped—but it was more than that. The silence that enfolded the darkening room was more pervasive, more significant. Half-consciously, he went over to the window and looked out. He took one glance at the sky, which had become a dull slate gray as evening crept in, and had his answer. The rain was no longer falling; lasting the entire day, the steadily droning accompaniment to his thoughts had finally come to an end.

Dakota began to smile. Whether it was the break in the weather or something else altogether, he found, much to his own surprise, that he was being filled with a sudden surge of power. He returned to his previous reflections, only to realize that they no longer disturbed him. Whatever might happen, it struck him in a wordless burst of feeling, he would still be able to manage. The days would still come in their endless procession, he would grow older, stronger, wiser, life would continue to unfold before him.

He went back to the bed and hurriedly pulled on his boots, eager to get out of the confining room.

And even a few minutes later, when he stopped in the hallway between the doors of Garrett's and Layla's rooms and wondered whether Garrett would continue drifting across the land with him or decide instead to settle down with Layla—even this did not disturb Dakota's newfound vigor.

He was willing to accept either possibility.

Nine

A Stirring of the Blood

Before going on to the sheriff's, Dakota decided to make a short stopover at the Scarlet Palace Saloon. He wanted to test himself, now that this change had come over him, to see how he would react to the sight of Garrett and Layla together. But more than that, he wanted to let off some of his enthusiasm in their company.

The saloon was nearly empty when Dakota came in. The meetings were over; the shopkeepers had chosen, as dusk started closing in, to take Graham's advice and go to the safety of their homes. The few remaining customers were mostly old-timers, who would idle away the hours there as well as anywhere else, regardless of what was going on around them. As they were fond of saying to anyone who would listen, they had seen much worse in their time.

The owners of the saloon were there too, sitting with two men at a table off to the rear. A large cigar planted in the corner of his mouth, it was Tanner who, with his usual self-assurance, had been doing most of the talking. He had his audience, though not as large as before, but this did not prevent him from giving his opinions a good airing. For the better part of the past hour he held forth, pressing on with his attacks against the sheriff and outlining the plans of action he would have put into effect had he been in charge. And Jason Pratt was content to sit quietly at his side nursing a drink, leaving his wife waiting with supper while he listened to his partner's vindictive arguments. He had planned to return home earlier, but the conversation interested him—as most conversations did—

110

and, as usually happened when he got himself settled comfortably in this home away from home, he lost track of the time.

Dakota scanned the saloon, searching for Garrett and Layla, but did not see them. Disappointed, he was about to go back out the door when he noticed Ginger and Laura May at a table near the bar. With the exception of Layla, these were the two women who had interested him most the night before. And now they were sitting alone.

By this time on most days, in anticipation of the nighttime crowds, they already would have been dressed in their dance-hall costumes, ready for work, but this evening they were not. Tanner had seen the effect of the sheriff's speech on his fellow citizens, and knew that, as a consequence, business would probably be off tonight. A shrewd businessman who knew how to keep his losses at a minimum, he had decided therefore to give everyone but the bartender the night off—without pay. The women had complained at this, but Tanner, taking the sheriff's side for the first time, had explained that sacrifices just had to be made in circumstances such as these. He, too, was going to be taking a loss, and he didn't like it any more than they.

It mattering little to him what the women were wearing, Dakota paused at the doorway and quickly ran through the alternatives open to him. Then, not wanting to go directly up to them, but far from willing to pass up this opportunity to make use of his new resources of energy either, he made up his mind what to do. Casually, pretending to take no notice of them, he strolled up to the bar. He dug into his pocket and came up with a lucky silver piece he had kept with him for months. *Well, this is as good a time as any to part with it*, he thought with a smile. He dropped it down on the moist bar top and called for a drink. With the aid of the mirror above the bar's bottle-laden shelves, he then turned an inconspicuous eye on the two women.

But Dakota had gotten himself in for a little more than he had expected. For while he was standing there, trying to decide what his next move should be, he himself had become the object of a few people's attention.

"Well, if it isn't the sheriff's little helper," Tanner remarked upon first seeing the youth.

Jason Pratt removed his glasses and looked across the room. "Oh, it's Dakota," he observed in his usual absent way. "What's the matter, Marc? He's a good boy."

"Yeah, that's just what he is—a boy," Tanner replied sourly. "And that's who Graham got to help him."

"I'm sure the sheriff knows what he's doing," said Pratt.

"There's one way to find out, ain't there," one of the other men who was sitting with them muttered. Brutish-looking, his chest enormous, Vince Downey was the town's blacksmith.

A mischievous sparkle appeared in Tanner's eye. "You think you're the one to give it a try?"

"Yeah, I think so," Downey chuckled. He turned to the fourth man at the table. "What about it, Clem? You want to come along in case I need some help?"

"Sure, sure," drawled Darl Clemens, a lank, mean-faced idler who every now and then helped out at the livery stable. "C'mon."

Grinning from ear to ear, they rose together and started across the room.

"Do you really think this is a good idea, Marc?" Pratt said nervously. "We don't need any trouble."

"What kind of trouble? Relax, Jase, relax. Nothing's going to happen. We're just going to put things in their proper perspective, that's all." Tanner took a puff on his cigar and sprawled comfortably back in his chair to watch.

"Well, well, what do we have here?" Downey said as he came up on Dakota.

"Hey, watch what you say, Vince," Clemens told him with mock respect. "That there's the sheriff's new deputy."

Dakota fought back a momentary look of surprise. Slowly he put down his drink.

"The new deputy?" Downey went on. "Are you sure? You know, Clem, you can't go making mistakes about something as important as that."

"No mistakes about it. Sheriff said so himself. I heard him."

"No kidding? Funny, he doesn't look the type to me."

"Ask him if you don't believe me. Go ahead. Ask him."

"Okay, okay." Putting on a broad, friendly smile, he asked in a new voice, "Hey, me and my friend here are having a little argument and we thought maybe you could help us out. Are you by any chance the new deputy around here?"

"I'm working for the sheriff," Dakota responded, eyeing them steadily.

Clemens slapped his partner heartily on the back. "See? Told you so."

"I don't know, I'm still not sure," Downey said to him. "Most deputies I've seen got themselves a little tin star they wear."

"Well, maybe he's got it under his jacket."

"Yeah, maybe." He turned again to Dakota. "How about showing us your star, boy? We're still not convinced."

"That's right," the other chimed in. "You ain't supposed to be hiding it or nothing. We should be able to see it plain as day."

Dakota remained rigid, impassive. His gaze did not move from them.

"Well, if you ain't going to oblige us, I guess I'll just have to take a look for myself." Downey reached for the jacket.

Dakota took a few steps back as the oversided hand was about to touch his lapel.

"What's the matter, boy? I only wanna have a look."

"Why don't you just forget it?" Dakota said quietly. "I'm not looking for any trouble."

"What do you mean you're not looking for any trouble?" the blacksmith snorted. "Ain't that just what a deputy ought to be looking for? The way I heard, it's all part of the job."

"You know what I think?" Clemens cackled. "I think the sheriff made a mistake. He went and got himself a deputy who's scared of a little trouble."

"I didn't say I was scared," Dakota replied. "I'm just asking you to leave me alone."

"Sure we will, boy, sure we will—right after I've had a look."

In the instant that Downey again reached for him, Dakota whisked back the jacket and drew his six-gun. Downey's hand froze in mid-air.

"I don't like people touching me," Dakota said in the same quiet voice. He cocked the gun. "So if you don't want your hand blown off, I'd suggest you go sit down and forget the whole thing."

The grins dissolved on the two men's faces. Suddenly neither of them had anything to say.

"Haw, that's the way, kid," guffawed one of the old-timers sitting nearby. "You showed 'em. You showed 'em good, haw, haw."

"Come on, no harm's been done. Let's forget it, okay?" Dakota said, understanding the position they were in. But the two men stood there immobile, burning with rancor, unable to back down.

"Why don't you do what he says, boys? You found out what you wanted to know."

Dakota looked around as Ginger came striding calmly up to the bar.

"We've had enough trouble around here; we don't need any more." Stepping between the three, she entwined an arm around Downey and started pulling the massively built man away. She continued pleasantly, making light of the matter, "There's no need for any of this. We're all supposed to be here to enjoy ourselves, so why don't we do just that? The way things have been around here, we could all use a good time, right?"

"Hell, leave me alone, Ginger," Downey growled like a stubborn child, wrenching free of her grasp. He looked at his companion and snapped, "Let's get out of here, Clem. I've had enough of this place for one day."

"Yeah, I think you're right," Clemens said, shooting Dakota a sidelong look. "The air around here is beginning to smell pretty bad."

Side by side, their gazes averted from everyone else, the two marched out the door.

Dakota cast a short glance at the woman. It hadn't worked out exactly the way he had planned, but it looked as though he was going to get a chance to talk with her after all.

"Thanks, I'm kind of glad you did that," he said in a casual-sounding tone.

"I don't know that you have to thank me," replied the woman. "I'm not sure if it was you or them I was helping out."

"Either way, I wouldn't have wanted to see it go any further," he said, reholstering his gun.

"Why? Would you have shot him?"

"Oh, maybe. But only a finger or two."

Ginger laughed. After studying the sandy-haired youth a moment, she said, "You know, I think you probably would have."

Dakota restrained a smile.

"Look, why don't you come on over and join us?" Ginger offered.

Dakota looked in the direction of Laura May. Turned partly around in her seat, the young woman was watching him. When Dakota's eyes met hers, she smiled warmly, openly.

"Okay," Dakota said.

"Sure, it's better than drinking alone." Ginger took his arm and led him over to the table. She moved her glass aside to sit opposite Laura May, and Dakota, who found it difficult to believe it was all really happening, sank into place between the two women. He gave each of them a short look and a smile as Ginger started the introductions.

"And what's your name?" Laura May asked in a sparkling voice.

"Dakota."

"Well, Dakota, you did all right for yourself back there. It was a good thing to see," she said with a friendly wink that set Dakota's blood astir. Lowering his eyes, he managed a word or two of thanks.

"It doesn't take much to guess that Marc must have had something to do with it," Ginger noted coldly.

"No kidding," the younger woman agreed, darting an irritated look over her shoulder.

"Marc?" asked Dakota.

"Marcus Tanner. He owns the place," Laura May explained. "And sometimes he acts as if he owned all the people in it as well."

"Oh, I met him yesterday," Dakota said, following the direction of their glances. The cigar still rooted to his mouth, Tanner was now sitting alone. Jason Pratt had also deserted him, leaving a few minutes after Downey and Clemens had made their inglorious departure. Pratt had finally realized how late it was getting, and hurried home for dinner.

"What's the matter, don't you like him?" Dakota asked as he turned back in his chair.

"Marc? Well, he isn't exactly what you'd call likable," replied Laura May. "But I suppose he's all right in his own way. There are a lot worse than him, if you want to think of it like that."

"And some a lot better," Ginger added. "But that's enough about him. Why don't you tell us a little something about yourself instead?"

"I don't know, there isn't all that much to say," Dakota said, unsure what it was they wanted to hear.

"You could always start by telling us why you're working for the sheriff," Ginger replied with a coaxing look. "There ought to be some sort of a story there."

"No, not really. I just thought he could do with some help."

"But there are a lot of other people around here who could help. Why did you volunteer?"

Dakota had no desire to go through his reasons another time. Instead, he shrugged the subject lightly and said, "Well, I didn't see anyone else volunteering."

"And that's why *you* did?" said Ginger. When Dakota replied with a simple nod, she and Laura May exchanged glances.

"Then you're planning on staying in New Eden for a while?" asked the younger woman.

"No, I'm just passing through."

"You mean you're not even going to be living here and you want to get involved in all this?"

"Like I said, someone has to help. Why? Is there something wrong with that?" he asked, questioning their expressions of surprise.

"No, not at all," laughed Ginger. "Far from it."

Dakota wasn't certain why it was, but he couldn't have hoped for things to turn out better. No matter how he answered their questions, he didn't seem to be able to do anything wrong.

And then something happened to disturb Dakota's mo-

116

ment of triumph. With the end of the rain, a number of the hands from the nearby ranches, having heard nothing of the murders, had made their way to town and started coming into the saloon. In his glory, Dakota took no notice of the men—until one of them, a tall, rugged-looking fellow, came swaggering up to the table.

"Hey, Laura May, how're you doing?"

"All right, Johnny. And yourself?" she answered casually.

"Okay, okay. But I'd sure be a whole lot better if you came over and joined me a while."

Dakota stared at him coldly. He hated everything about him, most of all his arrogance.

"I'm not working tonight, Johnny," Laura May said with apparent indifference.

But that did not stop the man. "So how does that matter? We can still try to enjoy ourselves, can't we? I don't think either of your friends would mind if I took you away from them."

Dakota was about to say something, but Ginger, seeing this, softly touched his arm and shook her head.

"Come on, I'll buy you a drink and we'll talk over some of the old times. It's been a while," Johnny pressed on. "And maybe we'll even have some fun while we're at it. Come on."

Laura May took a moment or two to keep him in suspense and then gave in. "Oh, all right," she said lazily, and rose.

"See you later, Dakota, okay?"

"Sure," the youth said quietly, and Laura May went off with Johnny.

Dakota watched them cross the room and take a table off in a corner by themselves. He recognized the smile that appeared on Laura May's face as she fell into conversation with the ranch hand. Warm and sparkling, it was the same one she had granted him earlier. Dakota's heart sank. He pushed away his drink and murmured, "Well, I think I'd better be going."

Ginger had been following his reactions. She had a good idea of how he must have been feeling. "Are you sure you wouldn't want to talk a little longer?" she asked, hesitant to say more.

"No, I don't think so. I told the sheriff I'd be there by now."

"Okay, then I guess you ought to," Ginger said. "But before you do, I'd just like to say that I enjoyed meeting you. And I'm sure Laura May did also."

"Thanks, I enjoyed it too," Dakota replied impassively. He got up from the chair.

"And, Dakota . . ."

Already moving away from the table, he stopped and slowly looked up.

Ginger flashed a broad, encouraging smile. "Good luck, Dakota. And give 'em hell. I know you can."

Dakota paused, held by the sympathetic look in her eyes. Then he, too, managed a smile.

"Thanks again."

Dakota found no one there when he entered the sheriff's office. After a quick look in the back, he settled himself into one of the chairs and waited. He closed his eyes and reviewed his experiences with the two women. Gradually he came to the conclusion that he hadn't done so badly after all.

He had been there only a few minutes when the door opened.

"Well, there you are," Jack Graham called. He remained at the threshold, leaving the door open.

"Where were you?" asked Dakota, his spirits suddenly rising. "I thought I'd find you here."

"Oh, I couldn't sleep. So I figured I'd walk around and keep an eye on things."

"Funny, I couldn't sleep either."

The man's gaunt face folded back in a smile. "Do you have an appetite at least?"

"Sure thing. You know, what with everything else, I almost forgot about that."

"Then come on, we'll go have ourselves a bite to eat," Graham said, waving him outside. "And you can have as much as you want. You're on the town's payroll now. They'll be paying for it."

Dakota held himself tall and proud as he walked down the street at the sheriff's side. All his doubts had finally

118

dissolved. He knew he was on the right path, regardless of what might happen with the coming of nightfall. And in case his confidence faltered, he could think of Ginger's parting words and they would be sure to restore it. No matter how many times he repeated them to himself, they always produced the same satisfying glow.

Ten

Six Cans of Peaches

The two figures stood alone in the center of the street. A pale, starless sky watched over them. The time had come.

"We'll split up here. You take that end of town and I'll go up this way. We'll meet back here every half hour, which should give us enough time to make a complete circle. If you run into any kind of trouble at all, fire off a shot. I'll do the same."

"Okay, I will," responded Dakota.

"Now I don't think I have to warn you against being trigger-happy, but I will anyway. The last thing we want is to have any innocent people getting shot. But on the other hand, if you run into anyone who looks the least bit suspicious, you get him to stop any way you have to. And remember to fire off that signal. I won't care who it is, I'm going to want to question him. No one's above questioning, and I mean *no one*. Especially if they give you any back talk. You'll have to judge the situation for yourself, but if you go by your instincts you should do all right."

"Don't worry, I'll know what to do."

The sheriff paused and studied the light-haired youth. "You know, it's not too late to back down if you want to," he noted soberly. "Are you having any second thoughts about all this?"

Dakota shook his head. "No, not at all."

"All right, good enough. Then here—," he said, reaching inside his coat, "—you'd better take this. It'll let people know which side you're on."

He dropped a silvery deputy's badge into Dakota's hand.

Dakota examined it a moment, then pinned it to his jacket. There might have been a time when it would have been a cause for excitement and pride, but now he had other things on his mind.

"We'll do without all the ceremonies. For better or worse, you can consider yourself deputized," said Graham, who, wondering one time too many why he was working for the townspeople, had come to regard his position with more than a touch of irony.

Hiding his concern for the youth, the older man tossed off a peremptory "You ready?"

Dakota nodded.

"Okay, then let's get going." Then, as they were about to part, Graham found himself adding, "You watch out for yourself now, you hear me?"

"And you do the same, sheriff."

The look of stony self-composure gave way to a smile as the man replied, "The name's Jack."

With a last glance that expressed all they had left unspoken, they went their separate ways.

Never more alone than he was now, Dakota walked past empty stores, crossed darkened alleyways. The rain had turned the streets into a heavy, slowly thickening mud that sucked at his feet, pulling him down with the weight of his own steps. Life seemed to have fled indoors, leaving the world around him in the hands of an oppressive, all-engulfing stillness.

Alert, trying to penetrate the veil of night, his eyes were constantly on the move. Blackened windows and doorways became potential sources of danger, and had to be watched; a vague shape nestled in the shadows required closer inspection before he recognized it as a rain barrel that had tipped over; every turn loomed up before him with the threat of the unknown. He began looking at the townspeople's homes in a way he never had before. Cozy, well-lit, they appeared to him as great fortresses of safety and security. But he walked on, shutting out any longings he might have had.

It was only when he reached the outskirts of town and gazed at the darkened mass of countryside stretching off to meet the heavens somewhere in the distance that he allowed himself a moment for regrets. Out there—he mused with a pang of emptiness—that was where he belonged. Out there the days were full and exciting, each one different from the next; the nights were welcome for the rest they brought, their stillness anything but threatening. And most of all—and it was on this that all his other thoughts centered—out there he was free to roam.

With a sigh, he turned and started back.

He felt a breath of relief when he rounded a corner and saw Jack Graham waiting for him at their meeting place. Drawn to him by the bond of the danger they both shared, he quickened his step.

"See anything?" the sheriff called as he approached.

"No. What about you?"

"Same here." Graham waited until Dakota reached him and then asked in a serious voice, "Are you doing all right?"

"Sure. It just gets a little spooky every now and then, but I'm okay."

"I don't know why I asked; I didn't really expect you to say anything else," the man said with a quiet chuckle. "But if it'll make you feel any better, it's the same with me."

They exchanged a few additional remarks to put each other at ease before Graham came up with the inevitable question.

"What do you say? You ready to go around another time?"

Dakota nodded, and once again he was off on his own.

But he had not gotten down the length of the first street when he saw something which made this circuit of the town even more difficult than the first. As he was passing the Scarlet Palace Hotel he noticed Layla standing by the window of her second-floor room. He waved, thinking she had seen him, but she moved away from the curtains. Dakota watched expectantly, hoping to catch her attention if she returned. Perhaps it was only to put his bravery on display, but he would have liked to have at least exchanged a smile with her. It would have brought a little warmth to a desolate night.

He waited less than a minute, and then the surprise

came. Instead of her, and appearing for only the briefest instant, Garrett went past the window. Dakota lowered his eyes. He didn't want to see any more; he felt lonely enough as it was. Garrett had his own life to lead, he knew, and there was little he could do to change hard fact. But he knew as well that he couldn't afford to dwell on this. Not if he didn't want to be caught off guard.

Dakota shifted his gaze to the shadowy streets and continued on his way.

The hours passed slowly and uneventfully. Jack Graham and Dakota had little to report to each other when they met. They rarely ran across anyone, and these few were far too wary and nervous to be counted as suspects. Whether out of fear or otherwise, the townspeople were keeping close to their homes.

It was only in the vicinity of the Scarlet Palace Saloon that there was any real activity, though even here things were quieter than usual. The sheriff kept an eye on the customers going in and out, but here, too, he found no one to arouse his suspicions. Unlike the majority of townspeople, the men who came in to the saloon on this night were not settled into the life of home and family. Men of the saddle and bottle, they lived where there was work to be found, if they wanted to find it at all; their days passed without a plan for the future. They led hard, uncomfortable lives, lives that often put them in close touch with violence. Had the day's weather been better, had more of them found themselves with money in their pockets, the saloon would in all probability have been more crowded tonight than it actually was. These men were not the type to concern themselves with meaningless acts of murder; no more than they were the type to commit them.

After making the rounds a third time and still finding nothing, Graham suggested they go indoors for a while. No less weary and dispirited, Dakota quickly agreed to the idea. They went back to Graham's office and dropped into a pair of chairs around the desk. For the chill in their bones, the sheriff produced a bottle and two glasses from the desk's bottom drawer; but for the raw sting of discouragement and failure there was no remedy to be offered. They sat quietly, drinks in hand, their legs sprawled wearily across the floor. There was little to be said. They each felt walled in by uncertainty, and there was no point in commenting on the little they already knew.

"Well, do you still feel like going on with this?" Jack Graham said after a long silence.

Dakota looked at him. "I'm not giving up yet."

"There's a chance nothing will happen tonight," the man pointed out.

"And maybe something will," Dakota answered quickly. "And there's no way I'm not going to be around if it does."

Graham smiled at his stubbornness. "Tell me, are you still going on that hunch of yours?"

"Oh, I don't know," Dakota said with a gesture of despair.

"Something change your mind?"

"What's there to change my mind? Nothing's happened one way or the other."

"Yeah, I've kind of noticed that myself," Graham said, chuckling grimly. "That's just the trouble, isn't it."

"You can say that again," Dakota replied, he, too, finding it better to smile.

Growing increasingly restless, they finished their drinks and went out again. They both agreed that it was preferable to be doing something, however little it might turn out to be worth in the end. Sitting still only brought doubt and uneasiness closer to the surface.

The sheriff did not vary the route he took. Each time he went up the store-lined main street, out toward the north end of town, where stood the homes of New Eden's more prosperous citizens. Each time his steps brought him to the fated site where, until only yesterday, the doctor's home had been. Making his fourth, and last, trip past this scarred gap in the line of peaceful dwellings, Jack Graham paused to contemplate the lifeless scene. Scattered across the soggy earth, the charred skeleton of the house loomed nakedly before him, an unsettling reminder of the event that had marked the beginning of the town's troubles.

Graham was thinking how the day's rain had added to the complexity of the situation, making it impossible to sift through the debris for clues, when the stillness was broken. He whirled. His eyes darted warily about, and then fastened on the source of the noise. An upper-story window of the neighboring house was being opened. Crouching, his gun already drawn, Graham waited for the lamp-lit figure to make the first move.

"It's all right, sheriff, there's nothing to worry about. It's only me," a woman called in a cheery voice.

Graham straightened his stance, recognizing her. It was Mrs. Rutherford, an eccentric old woman who lived alone with a houseful of cats she doted on as family. Graham sank his gun back into the holster and went over to the window.

"I hope I didn't startle you, sheriff. I saw you passing, and I wanted to find out if you caught that awful murderer yet," she explained as one of her cats, a slinky black creature, leapt up beside her and arched its back against the sill.

"No, I can't say I have. He's still out there somewhere," replied the sheriff.

"Well, don't let that discourage you any," she told him in a kindly tone. "You just go on with your job like you've been doing and I'm sure you'll find him."

Laughing quietly to himself, Jack Graham thanked her. It was good to see that at least one of the townspeople had confidence in him.

"And if you need anything, anything at all, you just let me know," Mrs. Rutherford went on. "Perhaps you're a little chilled? I could fix you a nice hot drink if you'd like."

"No, thanks again, but I don't think so."

"I understand, you can't spare the time," she said with an all-accepting smile. "But if you change your mind, don't hesitate to call on me. Whatever time it is, don't give it another thought. I'm willing to help in any way I can. After all, it's the least I can do. At times like this we all have to pitch in and do our share."

Graham nodded agreeably to everything she said, all the while trying to find a way to extricate himself from the conversation. But the lonely woman, eager to take part in the situation, chatted on.

"Isn't it just terrible, sheriff? I tell you, it's reaching a point where a person just isn't safe anywhere."

"Don't worry; you should be all right if you stay inside," Graham answered patiently.

"Oh, I'm not worried. I'll be staying right here at this window. No one will be able to come this way without me seeing them. I'm going to be on my guard."

"Good, you do that. That's a fine idea," the sheriff said, starting to back away. "Well, I'd better be going now. I've got a lot of ground to cover."

"Yes, yes, to be sure. But mind you, don't forget what I said."

"I won't."

With a cheerful wave good-bye, Mrs. Rutherford shut the window and returned to her rocking chair.

"You know, Homer, that sheriff's a nice man," she said, turning to her favorite cat. "I wonder if everyone around here appreciates the job he's doing."

The black cat stared at her with wide, unblinking eyes.

As had happened the three previous times, the sheriff returned from his rounds a few minutes before Dakota did. Wandering over to the hitching post that stood before his office, Graham was about to lean back and make himself comfortable for the wait when he stopped in midstride and turned. He thought he had heard something coming from one of the stores across the street. The six-gun at his side was again quickly in his hand.

He found the door to the general store unlocked. Cautiously, he pushed it open. He remained at the threshold and peered in, but could see nothing. The room was cloaked in darkness. And silence. He took a few steps inside. His eyes gradually accommodated themselves to the blackened surroundings. He was just beginning to make out the outlines of the shelves and counters when he heard the noise.

It was a low, uneven rustling sound.

Graham stopped where he was and listened closer. The rustling grew louder. It was coming toward him. He reached inside his jacket for a match. His fingers kept a steady grip on the six-gun. Then, a few feet before him on the floor, one of the shadows seemed to move. He struck the match.

In the first flare of melting phosphorus, Jack Graham saw the blood-soaked body of a man inching his way forward on his stomach. His back was shredded with knife wounds. The crawling movements he made were painfully deliberate, like those of a turtle. The little life that had not yet seeped from him was all that was pulling him on.

With a fitful effort, the man raised his face toward the flickering glow. Jack Graham went numb in that short, chilling instant of recognition. It was Lou Gardner, the dull-witted assistant to the already murdered store owner. He looked up at the sheriff with glassy, vacant eyes, the eyes of an animal incapable of comprehending its wounds. His lips, smeared with blood, slowly parted.

"Please . . . please help me."

The dimming flame burned at the sheriff's fingers, recalling him to action. He dropped the match, slapped the pistol back into its holster and hurriedly moved forward.

"It's all right, Lou. Take it easy," he said, crouching down in the darkness. "Can you hear me? It's Sheriff Graham."

"Sheriff . . . sheriff . . ."

"Just take it easy," Graham repeated. "Everything will be all right." Carefully, he turned the man over on his back. He pulled off his jacket and, quickly bundling it up, placed it under Gardner's head. He then struck another match, spotted a lamp resting on a counter in the back, and went over to light it.

"I never saw him, sheriff. I never saw him," the heavyset man groaned, unaware that the sheriff had moved away.

"Forget it, Lou. That doesn't matter now." Returning with the lamp and a piece of cloth to dab away the blood from his face, Graham sank down at his side. He could see that, having made Gardner as comfortable as possible, there was little else to be done. Even had the town's doctor been alive, he would not have been able to help him.

Gardner blinked up at the light. He turned his face toward the sheriff. "It happened too quick," he whispered. "I never got to see him."

"How long ago was it?" Graham asked, hoping at least to extract some bit of information to go on.

"Oh, I don't know, I don't know," Gardner answered through a heavy sigh. With the first slash of the knife, time had ceased to exist for him.

He breathed another heavy sigh. His eyes closed. Graham thought he had lost him. But after a long moment, Gardner's eyelids again fluttered open. A strange look, bordering on a smile, appeared on his tormented features.

"Six cans of peaches . . ."

"What?" asked Graham. He leaned closer.

"Remember, sheriff, remember how you asked me if he stole anything last night after he killed Mr. Johnson? And remember how I said I couldn't tell for sure?"

"Yes, Lou. I remember."

"It took me the whole day to look at everything, but I finally got it figured out. Six cans of peaches—that's what he took, sheriff. That's all that was missing."

The twisted smile widened. He was pleased with his accomplishment. Very pleased.

"You know what I figured then, sheriff?" Gardner said with a pride only he could understand. "I said to myself, Lou, this fella must really like peaches if he'd go and kill Mr. Johnson just to get a hold of some for free. Sooner or later he's gonna be coming back for more."

On the verge of blacking out, Gardner paused, fighting for air. Then, seemingly unconscious of the lapse, he continued, "So I went and got some cans from the back and put them right in the window. I figured that way he'd be sure to see them. All I had to do then was sit back and wait for him to show up."

As though recoiling from the conclusion of the story, he stopped again. Jack Graham contemplated him with a look of profound sadness. Only a half-wit could have come up with a line of reasoning like that. And what was worst of all, he had turned out to be right.

"You should have come and told me about it, Lou," he said quietly.

Growing suddenly anxious, Gardner tried to sit up. "You—you mean I didn't do good, sheriff?"

"No, you did fine," Graham responded, forcing a smile. He gently pushed the man back to the floor. "You did real fine."

Gazing at the sheriff with childlike trust, Gardner sank down against the jacket. The corners of his lips began to twitch sharply. His chest rose and fell with short, fitful breaths. He shivered with cold.

"Sheriff?" he called out fearfully, trying to penetrate the onrushing darkness.

"It's all right, Lou. I'm right here."

"I—I wanted to be the one to kill him," he said quickly, between painful pants. Tears were welling up in his eyes. "He killed Mr. Johnson and—and I wanted to kill him. Mr. Johnson was my friend, my only friend. He gave me a job when no one else would."

"Yes, I know, I know. . . ." Graham searched for a consoling word to offer, but nothing seemed appropriate. And Gardner was past hearing him anyway.

"I woulda killed him. I woulda killed him for sure. But it—it happened too quick. He came up from behind or something. I never saw him, sheriff. I never—"

Gardner shuddered. His eyes and mouth sagged open. The spreading chill, moving steadily up through his limbs, had finally reached his chest.

Jack Graham winced. Slowly, as though the life had drained from him as well, he removed the jacket from under the man's head and draped it over his face.

"Dammit!" he snarled through gritted teeth. "What the hell's going on around here?"

Graham pulled himself to his feet. Turning for the door, he drew his gun, trudged out to the porch and fired a shot into the air. Rooted woodenly to the spot, he scanned the long line of shops. Everything was as seemingly peaceful as before. He rubbed his eyes and temples exhaustedly.

Dakota was coming up from the other end of the street when he heard the signal. Pausing only for the moment it took for him to snap up his gun, he broke off at a run.

But he was not the only one to come rushing over to the general store. Filtering out of the saloon, curious to learn what had happened, a group of men followed closely at his heels. And, as could be expected, Marcus Tanner was among them, marching in the lead. With a strange placidity, Jack Graham stood by the porch railing and watched their approach. This latest turn of events, as incomprehensible as the others, had left him numb.

"What happened?" Tanner demanded in his usual authoritative tone, pushing past Dakota.

Graham looked at him with cold, impassive eyes.

Seeing that the sheriff wasn't about to answer him, Tanner went inside to have a look for himself.

"Was someone else murdered?" Dakota asked quietly as he came up to Graham's side.

"Yeah, that's just what happened," said the man.

"Did you see who did it?"

The sheriff shook his head distractedly.

"But you're all right, aren't you?"

The question brought Graham out of his thoughts. He turned to the youth with a weary smile. "Yes, boy, I'm all right."

Tanner came out of the store. The conviction that he had been right all along was written across his face. "Okay, so that makes another one we can add to the list of the dead," he announced in a voice laden with reproach.

Jason Pratt stepped forward from the group. "Why? Who was it?" he asked bewilderedly.

"Lou Gardner," replied his partner. "And I'd like to see someone convince me that *he* had an enemy in town."

The ranch hands began exchanging comments among themselves. Though they were certainly interested by the goings on, their remarks were free of emotion, remaining instead on the speculative side of the issue. Few of them knew Gardner in the first place.

It was quite the opposite, however, in the case of Tanner. As he saw it, the time had finally come for everyone to stand up against Graham.

"Tell us, sheriff, how many more people are going to have to be killed before you'll decide to let some of us help you?" he said loudly enough for all to hear. "Or do you still think that you and this kid here can handle it all by yourselves?"

"Don't, Tanner," Graham said in a low growl. "I'm not in the mood for it."

"I'm sorry, sheriff, but I'm not in much of a mood myself. This business has gone far enough. We've all got to do something about this, and we'd better start doing it soon."

Graham looked as though he were going to pounce on the man. He was long past caring what anyone's opinions were.

"I'm not going to say it again," he answered, slowly moving at Tanner. "Stay the hell out of this. I don't need you to tell me—"

Graham never got the chance to finish his warning. A single burst of gunfire, coming from somewhere at the other end of town, cut him short.

Everyone turned at once, frozen with surprise.

Graham spun around to Dakota. "Come on!" he called, and he and the youth darted away from the porch. The remaining men, not about to be left behind, followed hurriedly after them.

But by the time they reached the homes at the north end of town, everything had once again fallen still. They drew to a stop in the center of the peaceful street, not knowing where to go first. Only one of the people living in the area—most of whom were at their windows, watching fearfully—came forward to give them the help they needed. After telling his wife and children to stay inside, a thin, middle-aged shopkeeper anxiously emerged from his home.

"It came from over there! That's where the shot was fired!" he exclaimed, indicating the way.

Jason Pratt's eyes filled with horror. It was his home the man was pointing at. Overwhelmed by a fateful premonition, he bolted away from the group and started charging down the street.

"Hold it, Pratt," the sheriff shouted after him. "Don't go in by yourself!"

But Pratt heard only the voice of his own worst fears. He raced on.

"Wait, let me come with you!" Graham said as he and the others rushed along in Pratt's wake.

"No, *you* wait! All of you!" Pratt cried fiercely from his doorstep. "I don't want any of you in here, you understand? Leave me alone!" He ran into the house and slammed the door after him.

Trailing by only a few paces, Jack Graham heard the *snap* of the bolt being thrown into place. He tried the door, but it was locked firmly shut.

"Pratt! Open up!"

"Stay out of here!" came the shout from inside. "I'll shoot the first man who comes in! This is my house!"

131

With a sharp curse, Graham turned for the side of the house. "Some of you men go around that way," he barked over his shoulder, waving his gun. "Let's surround the place!"

To Jason Pratt, the rooms on the first floor looked as they might have on any other night. The lamps were burning, the table had been cleared of its dinner dishes, everything was neatly in place. All that was missing to complete the picture of perfect placidity was Mrs. Pratt. At this time of night, when she would be waiting for her husband to return from his place of business, she would normally have been sitting in a comfortable sofa in the parlor, reading a book she had selected from her collection of the classics.

"Janet! Where are you?" Pratt called as he scrambled up the stairs. "Janet, it's me! Where are you? Jan—"

The name froze on his lips when he opened the door to their bedroom.

But for the spreading bloodstain on the front of her dress, Janet Pratt looked as though she had dropped off to sleep in her clothes. The lines of worry that usually marked her expression had fallen away. Seeming more youthful than it had been for years, her face was calm. She lay rigidly atop the covers, her legs crossed at the ankles, her head resting on the pillow. The position of her right arm was all that disturbed her attitude of repose. Palm up, it was outstretched at her side, thrown back by the impact of the bullet.

The foundation of Jason Pratt's being collapsed in the moment that he saw the small pistol resting a few inches from the open fingers of her hand. It was his own. He had kept it around the house for emergencies. It was then, with that first paralyzing intimation of the full truth of what had taken place, that Pratt noticed the folded piece of paper that had been placed on the small table at the bedside. It was propped up conspicuously against the family copy of the Bible.

A hoarse wail rose in Pratt's throat. "No, God! No! Not this!"

With the slow movements of a man in his sleep, he crossed the room and knelt at his wife's side. He looked searchingly into her face. But he saw nothing, understood nothing. It wasn't really happening. It couldn't be.

As though groping in the darkness, he reached for the letter.

It had been written on Mrs. Pratt's finest stationery, in the neat, formal hand she used for all her correspondence. Carefully inscribed at the top of the page, even the date had been included. Pratt adjusted his glasses. With eyes lifeless and dim, he began reading.

My Poor Jason—

It is for you that I feel worst of all. I do not think that you will ever understand why I am doing this and I fear that it will haunt you the rest of your days. For your own peace of mind, you must not let this happen. It can do you no good. It is impossible to understand what goes on in the minds of other people, be it your wife or a common stranger. We are each locked up within ourselves.

The burden of loneliness has grown too much for me to bear. I thought perhaps you might be able to help, but I was wrong. Even tonight, with a murderer loose in our streets, you did not stay home with me. And this after our talk last night!

But I do not blame you, Jason. I have tried, believe me, but I cannot blame you. We each have our life to lead, and it is every person's responsibility to see that it is lived well. For my own part, I have come to see my life as a failure. I am not happy here in New Eden, but there is nowhere else for me to go. Everything will be the same, wherever I am. The terrible loneliness will follow me, I am certain of it. There is no help which you or anyone else can offer me. It was my weight to carry—and I could do it no longer.

Oh, how useless words are! They say nothing . . .

Good-bye, Jason. And remember, please, I feel no resentment toward you, none at all. Life is difficult enough; there is no need to search for forgiveness.

—Janet

Pratt put down the letter. He buried his face against the woman's cheek and began to sob.

There was a loud knocking at the front door downstairs. After circling the house and waiting five minutes for someone to appear, the men outside wanted to know what was happening.

Pratt rose from the bed. He folded the letter and placed it inside his jacket. He put the pistol back in the drawer of his dresser. Without looking back, he closed the bedroom door and went down the stairs.

He found Tanner waiting alone at the doorway. And behind him were the others. Men. Strange faces. The faces of people who would not understand, who could never know the truth.

Quietly, with all emotion set aside, Pratt said, "Janet's dead, Marc. Murdered in cold blood."

Marcus Tanner lowered his eyes from the man he had known since childhood. His sympathy for his friend was complete, whatever he might have thought of Pratt's wife.

"Come on, Jase. We'll go over to my place," he said. "You can rest there."

"I don't want to rest anywhere. Not until we've found the one who killed her." Pratt's lips trembled involuntarily at these last words.

"You don't have to worry; I'll make sure we get him," Graham put in solemnly. "But I think Tanner's right. You'd be best off right now if you went with him."

"So you think you're going to do everything just like before?" Pratt snapped with a sudden fierceness. "Well, you're wrong. This is my fight now."

"No, it isn't. Too many people have been killed already to make this a personal matter. Let me take care of it. That's my job," the sheriff told him calmly.

He turned next to Tanner and tried to reason with him: "Listen, why don't you take him with you? He doesn't belong here now."

"Don't trouble yourself about me," Pratt said in an attempt to appear natural. "I'm all right. I know what I'm doing."

"He sounds reasonable enough to me," said Tanner. "If he wants to stay, that's fine with me. It's his decision."

"He shouldn't be here, Tanner," Graham repeated.

The question of Pratt, however, had already become secondary in Tanner's mind. This was his opportunity; now was the time to make everything as plain as possible.

"Sheriff, I don't know what you're thinking, but it isn't going to be just you and that kid working by yourselves anymore. I haven't agreed with one thing you've done right from the start, so don't expect me to side with you now."

Graham breathed a weary sigh. "You know, Tanner, you're a damn fool. Let me tell you something: if anyone's going to be working with me, it'll be men I've picked myself. And you sure as hell aren't going to be one of them."

He glanced briefly at the people who had gathered there to watch and then turned for the door.

"If you don't mind, I'd like to see your wife. Where is she?"

"Why? What for?" Pratt asked. There was again a slight quivering of his lips.

"Your wife was shot, wasn't she?"

"Yes. But what does that matter?"

"That makes her the first one to be killed that way. All the others were stabbed," Graham replied, still patiently trying to measure his words for the bereaved man. "I think it would be a good idea if I had a look around. Maybe I'll be able to find something that'll help tell us who did it. You'd want that, wouldn't you?"

But that was the last thing Pratt wanted. He rushed to block the doorway.

"No, I'll tell you what I want," he shot back. "I want you to stay away from her. Enough's happened to her already. Can't she be left in peace?"

"Now look," said Graham. "We're wasting time. I want to be ready the next time something happens."

"And I said I don't want you going in there!"

"That's good enough for me, Jase," Tanner declared coldly, and before anyone could think of stopping him, he slammed the butt of his pistol down against the back of Graham's head.

"You've had things your way a little too long," he muttered as the sheriff sagged unconscious to the floor.

Tanner then smiled at his friend, "Don't worry, Jase, we'll find Janet's killer."

Dakota scrambled across the porch and knelt beside Graham—*his* friend. There was a moment of shocked

135

concern, and then he looked up. In one fleet motion, he drew his gun and cocked the hammer. "What the hell do you think you're doing, mister? You'd better put that gun down right now."

"Take it easy, deputy," Tanner answered, confident as ever. "Your sheriff will be all right. Now why don't you just put yours down? You're not going to use it anyway."

"Well if he doesn't, *I* will."

Standing off to the side, watching with the others, Garrett strode up to the porch. The sawed-off shotgun held a steady aim. Dakota beamed with relief.

"Go ahead, Tanner. Put it away."

Tanner flashed a sarcastic smile. "Sure, sure," he said, dropping the gun back into the holster he had strapped on for the night. "So what do we do now? Wait for the sheriff to come to? Or are you taking over now?"

"No, I'm not taking over," Garrett answered. "But I'd bet you'd like to."

"Well, someone had better. Listen, all of you," he then said, addressing his remarks to the wider audience, "we shouldn't just be standing around doing nothing. If we want these murders to stop, it's up to each and every one of us to do something about it. Now what do you say? Should we spread out and start looking?"

The men stared mutely. Tanner had miscalculated. It wasn't the same kind of a crowd he had spoken to from his bar-top podium earlier that afternoon. The ranch hands had come in for a night's entertainment; they were not about to get involved in the town's troubles, much less implicate themselves in the attack on Graham. The old-timers and their younger, but just as shiftless, counterparts were already thinking of returning to the saloon; they were not looking for any leaders. And the few respectable townspeople who had ventured out of their homes were well used to having the sheriff handle their troubles for them; they were in no mood for heroics.

Tanner's eyes grew dark and condemning when he realized they weren't going to back him up. "You mean not one of you wants to help? I don't believe it! Can't you see that Graham wasn't getting anywhere by himself? We're all in this together, all of us. We've got to—"

"Wait, let me . . ." Pratt interrupted. A strange, bitter

scowl knotted his features. The fuse of his guilt had been lit. He had come to believe his own lie.

"What's the matter with you people? You all knew my wife. What are you waiting around for? She was murdered! You hear me? Murdered! Dammit, that should be enough for any of you! Her murderer's out there on the loose, and we've got to find him. Find him and kill him! Now which of you are going to help me?"

When he saw the look in Pratt's eyes, a look he had never seen before in all the years of their friendship, Marcus Tanner began to realize that he might have sided with the wrong person after all. The crowd saw it too. No one said a word.

"What?" Pratt bellowed furiously. "Not one of you wants to help?"

It was a different sort of help that Tanner then decided to offer him. About this, at least, the sheriff had been right.

"Jase," he said quietly, "come on with me."

"Leave me alone!" Pratt snarled, shrugging him away. "If none of you will help, I'll go find someone who will!"

He turned angrily. Tanner tried to grab his arm. "Jase!"

"I said leave me alone!" With a strength derived only from madness, Pratt shoved his friend. Tanner went sprawling back across the porch. He stumbled over the sheriff's body and fell headlong across the open doorway. Rushing onward, Pratt tore through the crowd and started running from his home, the comfortable dwelling he would never see again.

"My wife is dead! Do you hear me?" he shouted hoarsely into the night. "My wife was murdered!"

The crowd watched, transfixed by the frenzied figure. They didn't try to stop him. They didn't dare.

Tanner dazedly hauled himself back to his feet. Emotions that had gathered over the years, accumulating into a brotherly love, came streaming to the surface. He began calling to Pratt.

Tanner didn't know that the past was already lost.

"If I were you I'd go after him," Garrett suggested. "You're probably the only one who can help him."

Jason Pratt was already turning the next street when Tanner hurtled away from the porch.

"Come out and help me!" Pratt called as he darted blindly through the town of his dreams. "I want my wife's murderer! Help me find him!"

The townspeople remained in their homes, peeking out apprehensively from the corners of closed curtains. They had no idea what the man was raving about, and they didn't want to know.

And gloomy, looming low, the starless sky watched indifferently over all. It, too, had no forgiveness to offer.

But there was always Mrs. Rutherford. Not stirring from her lookout, the aging woman saw enough, heard enough.

Alerted by distant, indistinct cries, she sprang to her feet. She saw someone appear a few houses away, at the top of the peaceful street. She could not tell who it was, but she could hear his latest cry:

"Please! Won't anyone help me?"

And then she saw the shadowy figure running after Pratt. They were coming in her direction, but Mrs. Rutherford was calm. She knew she had enough time.

"We'll help him, won't we, Homer?" Mrs. Rutherford said, and reached for the rifle she'd kept beside the rocking chair. Stealthily playing out her role, finally about to emerge from her loneliness to become a heroic member of a community that had long laughed at her, she drew open the window.

Mrs. Rutherford had been around long before Texas left Mexican hands. A veteran pioneer of the West, she had gotten her share of practice during the terrible and confusing years of the Indian raids. She was a deadly shot with a rifle.

"You must help me! My wife—"

Pratt was about to utter the words that might have saved his friend's life when the violent burst sounded. Nearly upon Pratt, reaching out to catch him, Marcus Tanner was struck in the chest. As though he had run headlong into a stone wall, he stopped short and reeled unsteadily in mid-air. He was already dead by the time he hit the ground.

But Mrs. Rutherford never got to see the effects of her aim. The impact of the rifle's recoil was more than her withered frame could take. The long-trusted Springfield slammed into her fragile ribs. The breath—her last—knocked out of her, she tumbled back from the window. Her head struck the edge of a bookcase and she slid limply to the floor.

Homer leapt devotedly to his mistress's side. One sniff was all that was needed for him to recognize the singular air of death. The black cat arched its head skyward and let out a piercing shriek.

The lonely woman had only helped plunge Jason Pratt all the more deeply into his lie.

Pratt had thrown himself to the ground at the rifle's explosion. Reflexively, he whirled and looked toward Mrs. Rutherford's window. But the woman had already met her fate. Then, turning again, Pratt saw who had been shot.

"No, Marc, no! Not you too!"

Already shattered by guilt, the distorting mirror of Pratt's mind quickly reassembled the scene into a new, less painful picture for him to accept. His gaze returned to the empty window. A vengeful grimace appeared on his face.

"Don't you fret, Marc, I'll get that murderer. He won't escape from me," he said with a feverish smile.

Mrs. Rutherford had made sure to lock her door securely that night, but that did not prevent Pratt from making his entry. Drawing his rarely worn gun, he fired twice at the lock, kicked open the door, and rushed inside.

Jason Pratt was certain of it: upstairs he would meet the person upon whom all responsibility rested.

The crowd had let Tanner go after his partner alone. They were disturbed by the change they had seen come over the meek co-owner of the saloon, but they had nonetheless felt it would be better to leave Pratt in Tanner's hands. They knew they wouldn't have been of much help anyway. Instead, they spent the few minutes that elapsed before Mrs. Rutherford made her mistake remaining where they were, gathered before Pratt's home. Their attention shifted back to the figure that lay sprawled across the porch. Baffled by all they had witnessed, they had preferred to wait for the sheriff to regain consciousness before taking any action of their own.

Keeping back the curious onlookers, Garrett and Dakota were doing what they could to revive Graham when the Springfield barked out its angry report.

Dakota's eyes flared with astonishment. The long hours, filled only with the unexpected, were beginning to have their effect on him.

"What is it, Garrett? What's happening?" he asked apprehensively.

"I wish I knew, boy."

After a moment's deliberation, Garrett made his decision. He rose from the sheriff's side and withdrew the sawed-off shotgun from its swivel holster.

Somewhat hesitantly, Dakota asked, "Do you want me to come with you?"

"No, you stay here with the sheriff. I'll take care of this."

A smile flittered across the youth's face. "All right. And, Garrett . . . thanks."

"For what?"

"You know. For being here. It helps."

"Forget it," said the man. "You just take care of your friend. And don't worry, he should be all right. I'll see you later."

With long, steady strides, his gaze firm and pensive, Garrett started down the street. Instinctively knowing a leader when they saw one, the anxious crowd followed.

They had little difficulty in finding their way to the source of the trouble. The two shots Pratt had fired came just when they could use them, telling them which way to turn.

Garrett was already standing over the body when the others caught up with him.

"It's Tanner!" one of the men exclaimed. "He's dead!"

"You think Pratt did it?"

"Why not? He could've done anything, the way he looked."

"No," said Garrett. "He didn't do it. He wasn't carrying a rifle."

He walked away. The narrow gaze was fixed on the open door of Mrs. Rutherford's home.

They found Pratt sitting beside the dead woman on the floor. The fire had gone out of him. His eyes were vacant;
140

his body was rigid. They flooded him with questions, but he said nothing.

They could only think of one way to explain what they saw. Mrs. Rutherford had been paid a visit by the same person who had killed Janet Pratt. And before making a hasty departure, he had taken Marcus Tanner's life as well.

Pratt, however, had drawn certain conclusions of his own. Yes, Mrs. Rutherford had been murdered. And then the intruder had fired at Tanner. But he knew something more than the others.

He knew that no one could have escaped past him. No one human, that is. There hadn't been time.

He knew that it was something more than any man or woman who was going through the homes of New Eden, claiming one victim after the next.

And he knew there was no point in trying to stop it, no point at all. He wasn't going to be foolish like the rest. Let them ask all the questions they want; he wouldn't lift a finger, he wouldn't say a word. Not him.

For after all, nothing would help. He knew.

The men searched the house, only to find Mrs. Rutherford's cats. But their turn had finally come; they weren't going to wait any longer.

"Come on, let's spread out," someone called. "One of us ought to be able to spot him and then he can signal for the rest."

"No, don't do it that way," Garrett said, holding them back at the door.

"Why? Do you have any better ideas?"

Garrett gave the man a look. He then said to the others, "You don't know where he is, so why go looking for him? We'd be better off if we could get everyone into one place. That way he'd have to come looking for us."

"Sounds good enough to me."

"Yeah, me too."

The others gave their agreement, and Garrett continued, "All right, then go out and pass the word to meet in the center of town. Let's say the saloon—that's as good a place as any. We can work from there. And make sure everyone knows, you hear? If they don't want to come, that's up to them. But they should at least know what we're doing."

The men filed quickly out of the room, leaving Garrett alone with the two unstirring victims. He went first for Mrs. Rutherford, lifting her from the floor and placing her on the bed. He then went back for Pratt.

"Come on, we'll go over to the saloon. You'll be safer there."

The devastated man seemed unaware of Garrett's presence. When Garrett attempted to help him up, his legs refused to support him.

"You can't stay here," Garrett tried explaining. "If you won't move by yourself, I'll just have to carry you."

But Pratt raised no objections. He knew better.

Jack Graham began to stir.

"Take it easy. You'll be okay."

The sheriff gave a quick start when he saw the figure crouching over him.

"Don't worry; it's just me," Dakota reassured him.

Gradually recollecting himself, Graham tried to get to his feet. He fell leadenly back against the porch.

"Why don't you give it a couple of minutes?" Dakota suggested. "You're probably just a little dizzy."

"Yeah, I think I'd better," Graham said groggily, and remained where he was.

His eyes darted past Dakota. "What happened anyway? Where is everybody?"

While Dakota was relating what he had seen, a few of the men who had been over at Mrs. Rutherford's came by and filled them in on the remaining details.

Trying to ignore the constant throbbing in his head, Graham absorbed the news with a tired, unflinching expression. He found it all too incredible to react any differently.

When the men had finished, he said quietly, "Okay, and what are you doing now?"

"Well, he told us to round everyone up and send them over to the saloon. He figured they'd be safest in town."

"Makes sense. Sure, go ahead. I'll be over soon," Graham said, and the men continued on to the next home.

"I think maybe your friend Garrett should have been handling this," the sheriff remarked soberly. "That's what I should've done right from the start."

"What are you saying that for?" Dakota answered. "You only did what you thought was right. There was no way of knowing how it was going to turn out."

"No, I suppose not, I suppose not," he said with a distant smile.

Once again, he tried to rise. "Come on and give me a hand. We'd better be starting back."

Layla stood with Garrett at the window. Behind them, the other women were clustered around a table, trying to bring Pratt out of his trance. The desolate man sat rigidly in his chair; in the five minutes that had passed since Garrett brought him into the saloon, he had not stirred from the position in which he had been placed. Laura May had wandered off to the other end of the near-empty hall and was sobbing bitterly to herself. Just as well as the others, she knew that the dream had come to an end.

"It's strange the way things seem to happen," said Layla. "Troubles never come one at a time. They always travel in packs."

"Yeah, I know," Garrett replied, peering out at the darkened streets. "Like yesterday, with the stage. How many people were dead before that was over?"

"Oh, I don't remember," Layla sighed.

The first groups of townspeople were beginning to arrive. They looked as though they were fleeing to the high ground from the encroaching waters of a flood. Men with their guns; women holding children still dressed in their bedclothes; others clutching the one or two possessions they weren't going to leave behind—they came in a steady procession out of the night.

"I wonder how they must be taking all this," Layla mused.

"We'll probably hear soon enough," said Garrett.

They turned to have another look at Pratt.

Ginger was trying to coax the man out of his stupor. "Come on, Mr. Pratt, you can't go on like this. We all

143

need you. We're your friends. You're more than just our boss. Come on, talk to us. . . ."

Pratt stared emptily ahead of him, alone in his broken world.

Ginger glanced up. "What's the matter with him? I never saw this happen to anyone before."

Garrett shook his head. "I don't know."

"But isn't there anything we can do for him?"

"I wish I had the answer, but I don't. His wife's death must have been pretty hard for him to take."

"I realize that," said Ginger. "But should he be acting like *this*?"

"Whether he should or not doesn't seem to matter," Garrett answered. "He *is*, and that's what counts."

"I have some salts up in my room," Layla suggested. "Maybe they'll help bring him out of it."

Garrett nodded. "It's worth a try."

Layla went off; the others returned to Pratt.

Stepping into her lamp-lit room, Layla was about to close the door after her. The feeling that something was wrong suddenly came over her, freezing her movements. A hand reached out from behind and clamped itself over her mouth. A second hand pointed a knife at her eyes. The backward kick of a boot closed the door for her.

"Make one sound, and I'll slit your throat. You understand?" a voice rasped in her ear. She tossed her head quickly.

"Okay, I'll let go. But remember: don't try anything. You won't live t' hear the end of your scream."

The hand dropped from her mouth. The knife pivoted around at her throat. The youth stepped out in front of her.

The words broke numbly from Layla's lips: "So it *was* you!"

"Sure, who'd you expect," Willy grinned.

Layla had seen the look of men bent on vengeance, but she had never before seen the utterly brutal fire that burned in Willy's eyes. It was more than vengeful; it was the look of a person who had given every fiber of himself into the hands of violence. He did not want to swim in blood; he wanted to drown in it.

144

"Stayed out of sight pretty good, didn't I?" he said, chuckling proudly.

In a voiceless whisper, Layla asked, "But why?"

"What's the matter, didn't you enjoy all the fun?"

Layla stared disbelievingly.

"Huh, I thought it was kind of a nice idea myself," Willy went on. "Just kill a couple of people here and there—that's all you gotta do. Then you can just sit back and watch the fireworks. It'll happen every time. People'll be runnin' scared and killin' each other before you know it. What about you? Didn't it make you just a little bit nervous?"

"Yes," answered Layla, "it made me nervous."

"Well, good, good. That was just the point. It wouldn'ta made sense if it was all wasted on you."

With Dakota at his side to brace him up, Jack Graham marched slowly back to the center of town. He was still reeling from the blow to his head.

"Well, we're right back where we started from, aren't we." he reflected sadly.

"I don't know, at least we're getting everyone out of the way so they'll be safe," said Dakota.

"That's fine, but what do we do then?"

"Start searching the town, I suppose."

"For who, son? We still don't have any idea who we're looking for."

Graham briefly contemplated a group of townspeople who were walking ahead of them. He smiled bleakly. "Who can say? Maybe the murderer's one of them. We wouldn't know. That's the worst part of it. It's all so damn senseless."

This last statement, which he had heard so many times before, struck Dakota anew. "What do you mean?" he asked. His expression had changed sharply. The same empty twinge he had felt earlier that day was once again gnawing at him.

"What do I mean?" replied Graham. "Well, I mean the murderer could be there at the saloon right now, just waiting for us with everyone else, and we wouldn't know the difference. We wouldn't know him if we saw him."

But Dakota barely heard his reply. Long passive, his mind had begun to work furiously. Kept in the background while his attention was occupied with other matters, the thoughts and fears he had dwelt on too closely during the day had been given a chance to rest and re-assemble themselves. And now they were springing forth, more forceful and coherent than ever.

First to come welling up from memory was a remark the sheriff had made: *A person can't hold a grudge against someone he doesn't know. He'd have to be plumb out of his mind to want to kill someone he hasn't even met before.*

Then something Garrett had said in Layla's room later that morning: *That's what senseless murders are. They don't have anything to do with the reasons you'd normally think of. It's murder for the sake of murder, nothing more than that.*

The final piece quickly flew into place. Dakota understood why Garrett's words had made such an impression on him: He himself had once wanted to kill. Anyone. Everyone. Murder for the sake of murder. The day he had wanted to avenge his parents' deaths. The day he had learned the grief that borders on madness.

The image of Willy—his nightmare, his grotesque double—leapt into his mind, and he knew. Outwardly groundless, the conviction was unshakable just the same. He knew with a certainty that surpassed all logic.

"Will you be all right?" Dakota asked suddenly, dropping his supportive hold on the sheriff.

Graham was interrupted in mid-sentence. Everything he had been saying had fallen on deaf, introspective ears.

"Why? What's the matter?"

"Will you be all right?" Dakota repeated.

"Sure, I'll be all right. But why—"

Dakota darted off without another word. He had to find Garrett—the one man who might understand.

Willy was slowly working himself up to a boil. The grin had dropped from his wolfish face.

"The people around here are gonna be real sorry you ever showed up in town," he was saying. " 'Cause you brought 'em more trouble than they're ever gonna know what to do with. A lot more of 'em are gonna be dead before I'm finished, a lot more."

Layla could only think of the same one question: "But why?"

"Why?" Willy snarled back. "What's the matter, you forgettin' or something? You killed—," his voice strained against the urge to shout, "—you killed my pa. You killed my friends. That was everyone I knew in the world. How'd you like that to happen t' you? Huh? Huh?"

The youth started moving at her. Layla stared. The twisted eye was close upon her. Deep within it she glimpsed the dark chaos that haunts dreams. She opened her mouth to scream, but Willy was faster. A hand flew at her. The punch knocked her to the floor.

Willy loomed down on her. Keeping the knife at her throat, he removed a wadded piece of cloth from his shirt pocket and stuffed it into her mouth.

"Now get up and come over here!" The grin reappeared. "Heh, maybe if you do like I say, I'll even let you live."

He yanked Layla to her feet. He wrapped a hand around her waist, pulled her to him, and started moving across the room.

A crowd had formed in the center of the street. Dakota came to a stop across the way from the saloon and began searching for Garrett. The man was nowhere to be seen.

Of itself, drawn there by a painful memory, Dakota's eyes skipped up to Layla's window. He saw figures moving behind the drawn shades. The two silhouettes seemed to be locked in an embrace.

Grimacing with thought, Dakota watched. Even after they had slipped from view, he stood there, battling with himself. He only had one conclusion to draw. What else was there to think? He had seen them before, and now there they were again. Garrett was more interested in Layla than in anything else.

But his feelings told him otherwise. His whole being recoiled from the notion. They wouldn't be there. Not now. Not Garrett. He couldn't believe it.

And he didn't.

Dakota broke through the crowd and ran into the saloon.

And there—just past the door—was Garrett. He was busy trying to calm down a group of nervous shopkeepers.

"What is it, Dakota?" Garrett said, catching the look on the youth's face.

Dakota did not pause to explain. He sprang past Garrett to the other end of the saloon and bounded up the stairs that led into the hotel.

He tore through the hallway and kicked open the door.

Willy was crouched on the edge of the bed. Layla was squirming under his hold. Her blouse was in shreds.

The bird-eye darted up. A look passed between the two youths, the two opposites of the same coin.

Willy hurriedly brought the knife back to Layla's neck and shouted, "You make a move, and—"

The blast of a six-gun cut him short. This time Dakota had not hesitated.

Hot lead gashed the twisted eye. Willy went flying from the bed.

Dakota scrambled after him, brandishing the gun. He stopped short. There was no need to fire a second time. The harsh features were barely distinguishable. Willy's face was drowned in blood.

Dakota moved to the bed and took the place Willy had occupied only a moment before. The woman lay there, still petrified. Though her hands were untied, she did not make a move to help herself.

Dakota removed the wadded cloth from her mouth for her and asked, "Are you okay?"

But Layla was beyond words. She vented her horror in a prolonged scream.

Garrett appeared at the door. The shotgun hovered in the air, seeking a target. Then, after pausing to take in the scene, he reholstered the weapon and strode into the room. He sat down on the bed, covered Layla with his jacket, and then gathered her up in his arms. Dakota watched silently.

"It's all right. There's nothing more to worry about. It's all over now."

As he spoke, Garrett stared at the corpse. Slowly, his

148

gaze moved to Dakota. He looked at the youth in a way he never had before.

Dakota responded with a grim, mirthless smile and got up from the bed.

Garrett's attention returned to Layla. "Yes, I know, I know," he said, gently rocking back and forth with the gasping woman. "Try not to think about it. You'll be all right now. It's all over. . . ."

A few steps ahead of some of the other, more wary townspeople, Jack Graham was the next to come rushing in. He had seen Dakota's expression; he knew to follow.

Graham stopped at the threshold and repeated Garrett's first motions. He then went to have a look at the body. After studying the twisted face, a face he had never seen before, he rose from the floor. He turned slowly.

"Is he the one?"

Dakota lowered his eyes. "Yes," he said quietly. "He's the one."

People began flocking into the room. One of them caught Dakota by the sleeve and asked, "Hey, you were here, weren't you? What happened?"

"Yeah, who was that anyway?" said another. "Why did he do it?"

"Leave him alone," the sheriff growled. "He doesn't know who it is. No more than I do. It was a stranger."

Dakota looked at him. The smile he had given Garrett returned to his face.

Graham began herding the townspeople outside. Dakota sank exhaustedly into a chair by Layla's window.

Everyone thronged into the hotel. Among the crowd that packed the hallways and lobby were the women who had been watching Pratt. With a last attempt at consoling their employer, Ginger and her friends had also gone off to see what happened. They had never thought he would move.

Pratt stared at the luxurious hall. For the first night since it had opened nearly four years ago, the Scarlet Palace Saloon was empty. Pratt's eyes registered what they saw, and this at least he understood: the dream was over.

Pratt got out of his seat and went out the doors. Eagerly awaiting news from inside the hotel, the townspeople had their backs turned to the saloon entrance; no one saw him step off the porch.

Not once did Pratt look back at the building he himself had helped construct. He had never really owned it anyway.

The man who had always dreamt of travel did not stop walking. Leaving the streets of New Eden far behind, Jason Pratt continued his slow journey into night.

Nearly an hour passed before anyone noticed Pratt's absence. Along with every other inch of town, they searched the hotel, thinking he might somehow have wandered upstairs to see what all the commotion was about.

It was while they were looking through the rooms on the third floor that they happened across the murderer's lair. Willy had taken refuge in one of the hotel's vacant rooms—the one directly above Dakota's. It had been there that he had spent the day resting his wounded leg. It had been the sound of his footsteps that had prevented Dakota from falling asleep that afternoon. Willy's father had long ago taught him how to find the best hiding spots.

There was no mistaking it: this was the place Willy had chosen. For there, scattered about the bedside, was the telltale clue—six empty cans of peaches. And on a table in the corner were six more, one of which had already been opened. Before going out on his night's adventure, Willy had made sure to replenish his stock for the next day.

Peaches were Willy's favorite food. He preferred their sweet flavor to everything, including meat. He knew how to hunt; he could have meat anytime he pleased.

Eleven

Further From Home

Wakefulness came with a start. Everything was dancing in rich, golden light. Returning from a long absence, the sun came over the horizon and travelled through a cloudless sky, brilliant, glowing. A cheerful breeze carried autumn's invigorating spell across the land.

The streets looked as they might have on any other morning. Brooms in hand, shopkeepers were cleaning out their stores for the new day; women scurried down the walks in groups of two and three; buckboards were drawn up here and there, waiting for a stock of provisions to carry back to the ranches. But for the Scarlet Palace Saloon and Bill Johnson's general store, it was business as usual in the town of New Eden.

Jack Graham strapped the pack to his saddle, undid the reins, and led his horse down the street. There was an empty spot on the breast of his jacket: he had removed his sheriff's star and left it behind in the office. He stopped before the hotel, retied the horse to the railing, and went upstairs. He had one last visit to make before going on his way.

A few moments after the first knock, Dakota appeared at the door. "Oh, hi," he said with some surprise. "Come on in."

He offered Graham a seat, but the man said, "No, that's all right. I just came by for a moment. I wanted to say good-bye."

"Good-bye? Where are you going?"

"Nowhere in particular. It's just time for a change," said Graham. When he noticed Dakota glancing for the star at his breast, he added, "A man shouldn't stay at one job for too long."

"You mean you've quit?"

Graham looked at the youth's flashing eyes. He smiled, recognizing his vanished past.

"They way I see it, a sheriff ought to like, or at least respect, the people he's working for," he explained. "And I don't think I ever have. Not that it's their fault or mine. They're just not my kind of people."

"Is that really why?"

"Yes, it is, son. It was interfering with the job I was supposed to do."

"I don't understand."

"Well, take yesterday, for example. If I *had* liked them enough to trust them, things might have gone a little differently. I might not have wasted so much time wondering which one of *them* had done it. No, I think they'll be better off when they find someone else for the job. I should have been moving on a long time ago."

"But you're not blaming yourself for the way it went, are you?" said Dakota. "Because I have more reason—"

"No, I'm not blaming myself. And neither should you. Whatever else you might want to think, don't go telling yourself how you were responsible. Because I'll tell you: when you've got trouble coming in your direction, there's nothing you can do to stop it. Everyone gets their share of troubles along the way. They never know beforehand, they always think they don't deserve it, but it comes just the same. This time it turned out to be a whole town that was on the receiving end, but that doesn't make a difference. It wasn't in your hands, or mine, or anyone else's, to stop it from coming. You should remember that."

Dakota responded with a bleak smile. "I'll try."

"Good, you make sure to do that. Believe me, I'll be doing the same," Graham said, sharing the smile. "And as for the people around here, they'll go on in their own way—without knowing everything. But they'll make out all right. There's something about them: they always do. I'd even bet they'll have themselves a new sheriff before the week's up."

"I'll take that bet. I don't think it'll be all that easy for them to find someone who can replace you."

"Thanks—but I think they're going to have to give it a try anyway."

Their expressions grew more relaxed. They contemplated each other warmly. There was nothing more to be added.

"Well . . ." Graham said at last, extending his hand to the youth. "You take care of yourself, Dakota. It was good knowing you."

"You still haven't said where you're going," Dakota replied. "Maybe we'll be headed in the same direction."

"Do you know which way you'll be going from here?"

"No, not yet."

"Funny," answered the man, "neither do I. But maybe sometime we'll run into each other anyway. We'll just have to leave that to chance, won't we?"

"Yes, I suppose so."

"And who can say what we'll be like then? You might just be the best gunfighter in the West, and me . . . well, it can always turn out you'll find me living a nice settled life. You know, a place of my own, a wife, some kids . . ."

"Why? Is that what you want?" Dakota asked suspiciously.

"Could be, son. Could be. Don't let anyone tell you any different: that's what everyone wants. It's just that some of us don't always get it."

Jack Graham gave him a wink and started for the door. But Dakota wanted to postpone their parting. "Hold on," he called after the man. "I'll come down with you."

On the stairs they met Layla, who was just returning from a short visit to the stage depot. Avoiding mention of the night's occurrences, the three exchanged a brief word and continued past one another. Layla went up to Garrett's room, where he was waiting for her.

The woman closed the door behind her and took a few hesitant steps into the room.

Garrett turned from the window. He asked quietly, "What happened? Is there a stage leaving today?"

"Yes, there is. But not from here in town."

"From where then?"

In a tone filled with irony, Layla replied, "Right back at the place we met."

153

Garrett breathed a cheerless laugh. "So what are you planning to do?"

"Well, the next stage out of here is the day after tomorrow. But I don't want to wait that long."

"Then you'll be taking today's?"

"Yes," she said softly. "I already asked them to make arrangements for me. It'll be coming through later this afternoon. I should have enough time to make it."

"Where will it be taking you?"

"It's going up north. I haven't really given much thought where I'll be getting off, though."

Garrett reflected for a moment, pondering her answers, his options.

"Would you like me to come along with you to the stage?"

"I was hoping you'd ask that. Yes, I'd like it very much," Layla replied. A smile appeared briefly. "I don't know, Garrett. I just don't know," she said with an empty sigh. "Perhaps I'm making a mistake, maybe we should be staying together longer. But I just feel—" She hesitated, searching for words.

"That's all right," said Garrett. "There's no need to explain. If it's a mistake, then it's one we're both making. We're in this together, you know."

Layla looked at him with surprise. "Then you feel the same way I do?"

"Yes, I wish I could say otherwise, but I do."

"But why is that, Garrett? Why can't we think it would work? It's terrible, but I just can't shake the feeling that it doesn't really matter how much more time we spent together. Whether it's another day or another week, it wouldn't make any difference. It would turn out just the same in the end."

"I know just what you mean," said Garrett. "But maybe that's because we're not in the mood for fooling ourselves."

"Why not, though? Don't other people fool themselves into believing it? For a little while at least?"

"Do *you* feel like fooling yourself?"

Layla tossed her head sadly. "No, you're right. I'm not in the mood. After these past couple of days, I'm not in the mood to fool myself about much of anything."

154

"Neither am I," Garrett echoed grimly. "Neither am I."

Their gazes fused. As one, they drew slowly together. They clasped each other tightly, clutching at the moment, never to let it go.

And then it was gone. Their lips separated, their arms fell, the emptiness returned.

"Tell me, Garrett, do you believe people ever really find what they're looking for?"

"No, not many," said the man.

"I know, that's the way I see it. It's strange, but I keep thinking of that girl from the stage I told you about. Over and over, I keep wondering: Was she running to find her man before the baby was born? Was she running *from* him, hoping to keep the child a secret forever? But in the end it didn't really matter. She never did get where she was running to. She died. The baby died. It all came to nothing. . . ."

"Garrett," she said with a sudden intensity. "I hope all our running comes to more than that. I really hope it does."

Garrett smiled. "Maybe it will."

Layla pressed her lips to his for a moment longer, then drew away. Silent, both knowing that the time had come to start their packing, they walked together to the door.

Layla stopped in the hallway and asked in a slightly different voice, "By the way, Dakota will be coming with us, won't he?"

"I'm pretty sure he will. He must be as ready as we are to start moving on."

"He won't mind? I know you were both planning on going further into Texas. This is a little out of the way."

"No, I wouldn't worry about that. I have the feeling he's learned not to bother much over plans."

A few minutes later, Garrett got the chance to see if he was right about the youth. He was getting some of his things onto the bed, when he heard someone coming down the hall. He thought he recognized Dakota's footsteps.

Garrett opened the door, only to find Dakota standing on the other side of the threshold.

"How'd you do that?" asked the youth. "I hadn't even knocked yet."

"Didn't you know I have good ears?"

"Yeah, I guess you do. I wouldn't ever want to have to sneak up on you."

Garrett smiled. Whatever else he had lost along the way, he had at least made one correct choice. If it was his lot in life to wander, then he couldn't have picked a better companion for the long, hard ride.

"So what's going on?" he asked. "What were you coming by for?"

"Oh, I don't know. I just felt like talking."

Dakota noticed the saddle-pack on Garrett's bed. He turned questioningly.

"Well, Dakota, how about it?" Garrett asked, preserving the same lighthearted tone. "You still want to leave town as much as you did yesterday?"

"What do you mean? Just the two of us?"

"Yes, just the two of us."

"But what about Layla?"

Garrett briefly told him of his plans to accompany Layla to the way station.

In response to the man's concluding question, Dakota said, "Sure, it's all right with me. But I don't understand. What happened?"

"Oh, let's just say we both decided it wouldn't work out."

"But it wasn't because of me, was it?"

"No, it had nothing to do with you. Take my word for it. Sometime I'll explain it to you. Don't worry, we'll have that talk you wanted. I know we both have a lot on our minds to say. But not right now, all right?"

Eyeing him with concern, Dakota nodded.

"Good enough," said Garrett. "Now come on, let's start getting everything together. We've been in this place long enough."

An hour after Jack Graham, the three rode out of New Eden. Dakota's gaze wandered off to the south, the direction Graham had taken. He wondered if he would ever see the man again. But he paused only a moment; he reined his sorrel around and followed Garrett and Layla's westward course. He knew this was the path he had to travel.

They rode much of the time in silence, often in single file. There was little to be said. The actions they had taken, the events they had witnessed, all had spoken clearly for themselves. Observations were unnecessary, casual remarks seemed out of place; conversation gradually yielded to the preferable solitude of watching a vast landscape slowly drifting past.

The sun had already crossed overhead when the way station came into view from behind a group of barren hills. Riding in the lead, Garrett reined to a halt and waited for the others to catch up.

"Well, here we are," he said with a bland smile.

"Yes, right back where it all started," replied Layla. A glance passed between her and Garrett; there was no point in mentioning how much had taken place since then.

"It's funny," Layla said, carrying forward the irony of the moment, "but the old woman said I'd be bringing back her horse someday. I guess she was right."

Garrett slapped the reins. "Yeah, I know. I was half expecting to see her standing there by the porch waiting for us."

But there was a reason Garrett's expectations had not been fulfilled.

When no one answered their calls, they dismounted and strode up to the cabin. Instead of the woman, the fetid odor of corruption greeted them at the entrance. They found Marta lying on the floor by the fireplace. Her dress was no longer its original black color. Before drying, the crimson stain had spread through the worn fabric. She looked as though she were clothed in blood. They recoiled from the doorway, repelled by the breath of decay.

"No, not again," murmured Layla. "It just doesn't stop, does it?"

Garrett put an arm around her. Slowly, they moved away.

Dakota turned to close the door. He noticed a piece of paper a few feet from the body, and released his grip on the handle. Covering his face, he went inside, picked it up, and hurriedly returned to the porch. He examined it a moment, then started after Garrett and Layla.

"Look at this," he said, displaying the timetable of stages. "This must explain how Willy knew where—"

He stopped, held by their expressionless gazes. Then he, too, understood.

"Yeah, I guess you're right. It doesn't really matter."

Dakota crumpled the paper and tossed it to the wind.

Garrett was throwing the last shovels of earth onto the grave when they heard the approaching rumble of the stage. He glanced at Layla, put the shovel down, and went with her to the front of the cabin. Dakota remained a short distance behind, letting them have a last few minutes to themselves.

Time flew from the grasp of the man and woman, rushing forward to the moment of their separation. As in a dream, events ran one into the next, never pausing to allow contemplation. The stage grinding to a halt, the driver's questions regarding Marta, the few passengers who got out to stretch their legs while the teams were changed—the scene unfolded before them, leaving them with little to do but watch and wait.

And then the moment came. The passengers returned to their places; the driver took Layla's carpetbag and stored it away; good-byes were exchanged. But this, too, was soon past. Layla took a seat with the other passengers, the door was closed, and all that remained were a last few waves from either side of the window. The driver climbed aboard and slapped the reins. There was a sharp yell to the horses, and the stage was off.

Rooted to the spot from which the last farewells had been uttered, Garrett watched as another vague hope receded before him, watched until all that could be seen in the distance was a billowing cloud of dust.

Standing off to the side by the porch, Dakota quietly came up to him.

"Garrett? Do you want to go now?"

"Want to?" answered the man. "No, not really. But I guess we should."

They mounted up, chose a direction, and rode on.

158

GREAT WESTERN ADVENTURE
FROM ⬟ AVON

ACTION AT ARCANUM
William Colt MacDonald   14332   .75

APPLEGATE'S GOLD
Todhunter Ballard   17525   .75

CAT EYES
Richard Brister   15065   .75

GUN SHY
Mitchell Dana   14779   .75

HIGH IRON
Todhunter Ballard   01438   .60

THE KANSAN
Richard Brister   15917   .75

THE LAST BUFFALO
Mitchell Dana   14522   .75

LAW KILLER
Richard Brister   16790   .75

LEAD RECKONING
Ray Hogan   18065   .75

THE MOONLIGHTERS
Ray Hogan   18879   .75

NIGHT RAIDER
Ray Hogan   18549   .75

PLUNDER CANYON
Todhunter Ballard   17673   .75

RENEGADE BRAND
Richard Brister   17152   .75

SHOOTOUT AT SENTINEL PEAK
Richard Brister   16519   .75

STIR UP THE DUST
William Colt MacDonald   04697   .75

TOWN WITHOUT A PRAYER
Mitchell Dana   04457   .75

WOLF STREAK
Richard Brister   15321   .75